HEATHER B. MOON

Lottie Saves the Turtles

Lottie Lovall International Investigator

For Louie, Amelie and Charlotte Rose xxx

Contents

Plastic, Plastic Everywhere!

Present Day

Plastic, plastic everywhere!
We really need to think.
What have we done to this world?

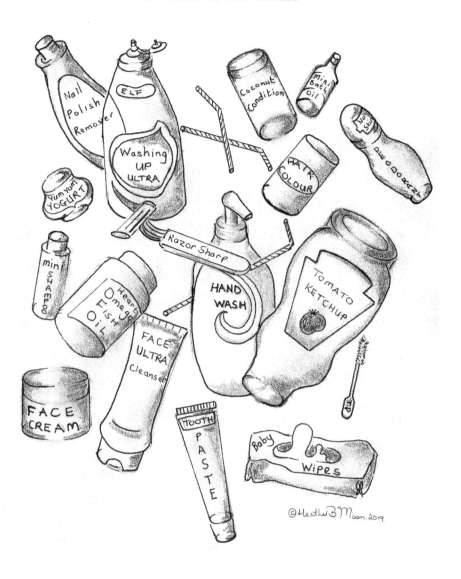

Perched on the kitchen bar stool, I gaze around at the plastic rubbish. I'd better help with the recycling routine. Plastic bottles, bags, tops, fruit containers and a drinking straw plop into the blue bin. **A drinking straw!** I thought my little brother Jack had more sense now. If I'd stayed at home in dreary Manchester I don't think I'd have even cared about it. But . . . I will never forget what happened to Timmy the turtle. I gaze at the glittering turtle magnet clinging to the fridge door.

Before my trip to the beautiful Caribbean island of Wadadidili, I'd never given much consideration to turtles. Of course, I've seen them on TV, and there are lots of pictures on Instagram. Jack owns all of the *Teenage Mutant Ninja Turtles* . . . Leonardo, Michelangelo, Donatello and Raphael, but they are just plastic toys.

Then the magic happened. Magic only occurs in Disney films and books, right? But here's the weirdest thing of all . . . it happened to us. Voodoo magic! I could **not** believe it. Not one little bit. Gloomy warnings of Turtle Island did not stop me though. There was no choice. Amy and I had to go to that creepy place. And when we faced a spine-chilling voodoo witch, a hairy man-beast, peculiar-Picasso-type kids, and fashionable living dolls, I had to believe in magic. Turtle Island is the spookiest place, EVER!

Yesterday I returned to rainy Manchester. I already miss the sunny Caribbean and the excitement of solving a serious case. That's what started it all. Something was extremely wrong. I had to trigger my detective skills and investigate. Maybe if I'd stayed at home I wouldn't have been aware that plastic can cause so much harm to sea creatures and I could **not** believe my discovery.

It was horrible!
It was bad!
It was evil!
It was pure greed!

I needed to make a difference. I hope I did!

Lottie Lovall International Investigator: Caribbean, Here I Come!

"Blooming, blithering bluebottles!" yells Mum, "I've sliced my finger with this *flippin'* knife."

Mum is having one of her creative language explosions again.

"What have you done now, Mum?" I spot a splattering of gooey blood dotted over the cream granite worktop.

"I'm trying to get into this *blinkin'* plastic packet," growls Mum. Sorry I asked!

"Well, why don't you use the scissors?"

"It's the *flippin'* new scissors I'm trying to open," yells Mum as blood drips from her fingertip. "Your dad lost the scissors and now I'm trying to open the new packet but they make it impossible to get in it."

Why is he always *my* dad when he's done something wrong?

"That's the thing with packaging, it all seems totally unnecessary," I say. "Everything is wrapped in plastic. Very tough plastic! Let me try, Mum." I take the package and use my nail scissors to get in. Crazy that you need scissors to get into a packet of scissors. I manage to free the shiny new pair from their plastic prison. "I'm off to finish my packing now," I say. I leave Mum as she runs cold water on her sore finger and dash upstairs to my room.

I'm so excited I can't wait for this trip. I will see Tristan and Katie-Louise again. My best friend Amy is sleeping over at my house tonight as we have an early start in the morning. It's a shame we can't go to the sunny Caribbean on our own and have some perfect girlie time but at least we're going together. It took some serious negotiation with the parents to persuade them that Amy could come too. Apparently, the Caribbean is mega expensive and we are staying at an *all-inclusive* hotel, whatever that means. We are meeting Nana and Pop at the *Royal Wadadidili Hotel* as they are flying from a London airport and we are flying from Manchester.

Zing-Zing! My phone zaps into action on the bedside cabinet. It's a WhatsApp message from Tristan. Yippee!

Hi Lottie looking forward to seeing u 2morrow. Katie Lou is working on the turtle project. There's defo a serious problem. We cud use ur help. The scuba diving is SICK though! See u at ur hotel 2morrow eve. Have a good flight, luv T xx

Ooooh! How exciting! Lottie Lovall International Investigator to the rescue. I do love a serious case to get my teeth into. My thumbs flick over the keyboard letters. I'm getting quicker at this – it's my new challenge along with my new phone app game, *Escape Week*. I'm totally addicted. Mum says she's going to confiscate my phone if I don't limit my time with it. The game is excellent for detective training. My reflexes are performing at breakneck speed since I've been playing. Super Brain Power! I've already reached level *B* for *BELOW*. I tap my reply to Tristan.

Hi T, Can't wait :) xx

That'll do for now. I need to do my packing as Amy will arrive soon. Once we start giggling, the packing will never get done. We do have a laugh when we get together. Amy is my very best friend. She is incredibly sensitive and can be a bit of a wimp at times but I love her to bits.

Me and my best friend Amy

Carefully folding a new top, my thoughts flip over to Nana. I love Nana and Pop. They sent me some money for new holiday clothes. I bought a T-shirt with pink and blue squiggly-patterned flower design, some new pink shorts and a pink bikini. Pink is my favourite colour but Mum says it clashes with my mad, red hair. I don't care much about 'clashing', I like pink and THAT'S THAT!

Popping my new clothes in my case I remember to put the bikini on top for easy access then ZIP! ZIP! ZIP! . . . I'm ready for a new adventure! Lottie Lovall International Investigator, Caribbean here I come!

The Island of Sea and Sun

"Where exactly is Wadadidili?" asks Jack gazing out of the window of the jumbo-jet.

"It's an island in the beautiful Caribbean Sea," replies Mum, who's sitting next to him.

"I can see it! Look!" I yell and swish around excitedly in my seat. Turning back, I gaze at the view below through the tiny aeroplane window.

"Oh yes, I can see the runway and lots of palm trees," says Jack. "Do you think this big plane will be able to land on such a small runway, Dad?"

Dad turns around and replies, "Of course it can, son. The pilot does this every day and the plane has automatic landing gear." Dad can be very boring when anyone asks a question. He goes on and on.

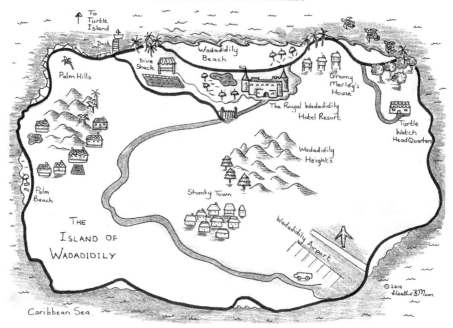

Mum puts her magazine away in her massive handbag.

"Soon be there," she says, "then I can change into my new red bikini and chill out on a sun-bed by the pool." She stretches out her legs and twiddles her ankles for the zillionth time.

My body does a jig-jog dance in the seat as the plane jerks, bumping and shaking along the runway. I love this bit. As the seatbelt signs are switched off, people immediately push and shove to be first off the plane. Everyone is herded through to passport control like a flock of sheep. We all wait around the baggage carousel, looking out for our suitcase to tumble past. People are pushing and shoving again to get to the front.

"I don't see why people can't stand behind the line. If they did, everyone would be able to see their cases and step forward to get them," grumbles Mum. A tall man drags his heavy suitcase off the carousel and knocks a little girl flying. She starts to scream the place down.

The next suitcase bobbing along on the baggage carousel is mine. The black and pink swirly design makes it easy to recognize.

"Aw! Missed it now," says Dad with a grumpy expression on his face.

"Oh, don't be in such a rush, Tom," says Mum, "we are on holiday you know."

It seems like a trillion years pass before all four suitcases are eventually on a trolley. Some awful 'Dad-scented' liquid is oozing out of a corner of Dad's case. We all stagger through the airport's exit doors. Dad's suitcase is leaving some horrid chocolate-coloured gunk in a wiggly trail behind him.

The heat hits me like a blast of central heating. I spot a pair of hands waving a sign up high in the air which says:

Welcome to Wadadidili
Live the Life!

"Is that our rep over there, Mum?" I point to the girl dressed in a Day-Glo orange T-shirt.

"Well spotted, Lottie!" says Mum. The girl's long, dark hair shines in the sunshine as we approach her.

"Hi there you guys – I'm Jo," she says in her American accent. "What's the family name, please?"

"Lovall," says Mum.

"Please make your way in that direction, Mrs Lovall. Your coach is number six and is parked in the shade of the palm trees." Jo points to a row of coaches and we all trek across the road. It's absolutely SCORCHIO. I'm melting!

Once the luggage and all the passengers are loaded onto the coach, it begins its winding journey through the Caribbean countryside. I see palm trees waving in the gentle tropical breeze as the bus passes through little shanty towns. Tiny houses are painted in bright colours: turquoise blues, lime greens, vivid pinks and sunshine yellows. Just like the colours on a paint chart at Homebase.

Skinny white cows graze at the side of the road. Each one has a large, white bird perched on its back.

"What are those birds doing, Dad?" asks Jack.

"They are a kind of egret bird, Jack and they pick all the insects off the cow for food. It keeps the cow free of parasites at the same time so they are both happy," replies Dad. He knows about these things. It's quite interesting, I guess. Soon the coach slows down as it reaches the entrance gates to a large building surrounded by lush, tropical gardens.

"This looks like our hotel kids – do you know it's all-inclusive? That means we don't have to pay for anything at all." Dad says. "All our food, drinks, entertainment and water-sports are included in the cost! We are going to have a *beefer*!" This is one of Dad's favourite words. He uses it when something excites him.

The coach approaches the huge iron gates and a guard waves it on. The sign at the front says:

'WELCOME TO THE ROYAL WADADIDILI'

"It looks fabulous!" yells Mum. "I can't wait to get around that pool in my new bikini."

"And I can't wait to get on that dance floor and bash out some moves," says Dad.

So CRINGE! It's going to be a long holiday!

Embarrassing Parents Syndrome (E.P.S.)

Everyone shuffles from the coach and we follow Jo, sheep-like again, to the hotel's reception. It's a huge room with squishy sofas. Mum flops down as she is offered a cocktail by a smiling waiter. I help Dad at the check-in desk and receive the room-key to our special family room. We turn to join Mum, who by this time is chatting to a podgy man standing beside her. He is dressed in a smart suit and is grinning at Mum. Racing-car cuff-links spark ruby-red flashes from his shirt sleeves.

". . . yes Madam, I am the owner of this hotel . . . have been for twenty years now," Podgy-man says. He turns towards me and does his beaming grin routine. His massive teeth remind me of the white traffic-barrier posts at the mall.

Dad gives him the grizzly-bear-face. He always does this if anyone strange talks to me or Mum. I suppose it's his fatherly way of protecting the family.

"Well, enjoy your stay and don't hesitate to ask my staff if you need anything. Have a nice day!" With that, the owner bounds off to the next person.

"Who was that?" grumbles Dad.

"He seems a nice man," says Mum, "he says his name is Hamish MacDougal and he owns this hotel. "

"Seems like a great bighead to me," says Dad with a huff. I agree with

Dad on this occasion.

I spot Nana and Pop rushing towards us. Nana is doing one of her 'Yoo-Hoo' routines.

"Yoo Hoo! Lottie! Amy! Jack! Jenna! Tom!" Nana shouts all our names across the reception area. I run to give them both a squeezy hug. "Oh! I've missed you." Nana crushes the life out of me.

Hamish MacDougal

Our room is lovely. The white walls are decorated with pretty flowers and hummingbirds. There is a large double bed for Mum and Dad in one half of the room with a single bed for Jack in the corner. A partition door slides open to reveal a small room with single beds for me and Amy.

"Epic!" Amy yells. We leap on the beds to test them.

"Look!" shouts Jack excitedly, "There is a little fridge here filled with drinks."

"Yes," Dad replies with a knowing smile, "that's the mini-bar and all the drinks are included because it's all-inclusive, you know." I'm already getting tired of Dad's constant reminders. I hope adult activities are all included to get the parents out of my hair. I open the patio doors to the balcony and step out to admire the view. It's jaw-droppingly gorgeous! The soft white sandy beach curves around the bay and the turquoise sea sparkles like a zillion diamonds. I can't wait!

* * *

Just then Mum's voice rings out in its usual bossy way.

"Come on kids, time to unpack and then we can all explore together."

I'm just about to hang up my new jeans when Dad's pneumatic drill of a voice blasts from the other side of the partitioned door.

"What the heck is all this sticky stuff all over my clothes?" he yells.

"Oh no!" Mum cries as she lifts a white shirt off the top of his case. The shirt has soaked up most of his gooey chocolate-brown hair gel. "I told you to put all liquids in a plastic bag. I don't know how it even got through security. Nearly all your clothes are ruined."

"I've still got my red shorts. They'll have to do for now," Dad replies.

Mum helps him unpack, placing the 'Macho-Cappuccino' stained clothing in a bath-full of cold water.

We all change into cooler clothes. Amy and I wear our new shorts and T-shirts. Mum is wearing her new red and yellow striped bikini, Jack wears a Man City kit and Dad, who is not so cool, wears a stripy blue shirt that managed to escape the hair gel crisis with his most ridiculous shorts. They are bright red and skin tight. He bought them in Newquay before I was born. They are older than me and they seem to follow us on every holiday. Parents!

"Right, where's the bar?" says Dad. "Let's go and explore."

We walk through the tropical grounds of The Royal Wadadidili Hotel, following the arrows that read, *To the Beach*. A painted hand-shaped sign points to *The Calypso Bar*. Waitresses and waiters are dressed in white uniforms and wander around handing out clean, fluffy white towels or cool cocktail drinks. At the edge of hotel there's a swimming pool surrounded by sun-beds and a large swim-up bar at one end. Exciting or what? It beats Blackpool on a rainy Bank Holiday Monday.

Mum settles on a sun-bed immediately, showing off her new bikini. UGH! Dad perches on a high stool at the side of the bar and orders a drink. He then bores some poor man about *what good value for money these all-inclusives are.* We need to escape and explore the beach.

I sink my toes into the sugary white sand and hear the splish-splashing of the frothy waves.

"Look Lottie and Amy! There're sea-tractors, jet-skis and a banana boat!" Jack shouts. "They look like fun. Come on, I'll race you! Last one there's a wally." He is already on his way to the exciting sea toys.

It looks fun. I ask the smiley attendant if we can hire a sea-tractor.

"There's no charge," he laughs, showing a gold tooth as he jangles his beaded hair. He unties a sea-tractor. We slip on our buoyancy aids and grab the sea-tractor.

It's such fun, peddling the blue floating tractor through the sea. We peddle in turns. First Amy and Jack peddle and I sit in the middle.

We peddle for an hour until our legs ache like mad and our faces are beetroot-red from the sun. My tummy is rumbling like a mini volcano. I realise I haven't eaten a thing since breakfast. Dad is waving at us from the shore-line shouting,

"Time for dinner kids, come on, it's all paid for, you know!" Ugh! It's going to be a long week!

* * *

After a yummy meal at the all-you-can-eat buffet we go to the Calypso Bar. Reggae music is blasting out by a band called 'Coconut Harlem'. The lead singer has long dreadlocks and about twenty gold bangles around his wrists.

"Come on, Jenna, this is our tune. Let's bash out some moves." Dad pulls Mum towards the dance floor. She does that 'dance all the way from your seat routine'. SO CRINGE!

Mum and Dad play their embarrassing parent act for some time. Dad waves his thumbs up in the air and Mum wiggles about in a shiny black skirt. I glance at Amy, roll my eyes and point to the games room. It's safer to leave them to it and have a game of pool!

©2019
Heather B Moon.

Tristan and Katie-Louise walk in just as we are setting up the pool balls. I greet them both with a big hug and Amy does the same. It's great to see them again. We had such a great time in Canario Bonito when we saved the baby dolphins from a life of captivity. Tristan's hair has grown so much since I saw him last. Blonde straggles flop into his eyes. Katie-Louise has beads in only one side of her hair now . . . so cool! She tells us about the work she is doing with the turtles here.

"It's an amazing job. We scuba dive every day and observe the turtles in their natural habitat," she says. "I'm also a member of Turtle Watch. We work to protect the turtle eggs in their nests."

Exciting or what? Imagine spending every day scuba diving and observing sea life. I feel an incey-wincey hint of jealousy.

"We'd love to go scuba diving again, Wouldn't we Amy?" I turn to my best friend and flash my widest smile.

"Ooh! Yes we would." Amy beams. The last time we went scuba diving was in Canario Bonito at half term. It was EPIC!

"We have booked a scuba dive for tomorrow afternoon if you're interested," says Tristan. "You may have to do a practise try-dive in the morning. We'll meet you at the Dive Shack at ten o'clock and I'll introduce you to Marcus the dive instructor. I'm doing my boat handling course so you may see me practising."

Yippee! Can't wait! And it's ALL INCLUSIVE! No need to negotiate with the parents this time.

Tristan and Katie-Louise

Live the Life!

The following morning I awake to a cloudless sky, hot sun and the most dazzling blue, blue sea EVER. Tumbling out of bed, Amy and I go down to the Sunrise Restaurant for the buffet breakfast. I like it here because we can do our own thing. Mum, Dad and Jack went for breakfast ages ago to meet up with Nana and Pop. They get up too early for us.

The tables are loaded with all kinds of delicious food. There is an amazing bar called '*Fabulously Fruity*', with exotic types of fruit such as mangoes, papaya, passion fruit and just plain old bananas. A chef is cooking omelettes behind another bar called '**Eggs U Like**'. The sign above the next table says, '*Lovin' It Hot Hot Hot!* ' – huge silver dishes contain sausages, bacon, tomatoes, baked beans, pancakes and mushrooms. There's also every shape and size of bread roll and sweet pastry on offer at the '*Baker's Corner*'.

We join the others at the table. They have all finished eating and are drinking coffee.

"What are you two planning on doing today?" asks Mum, "I've noticed there's a kid's club at the beach with organized activities on offer."

"We're meeting Tristan and Katie-Louise at the Dive Shack at ten o'clock." I say. "We want to go scuba diving. What are you all going to do?"

"Oh, that sounds good! I'm going to relax, relax and relax," replies Mum, "I've got lots of books downloaded onto my new e-reader to enjoy whilst I soak up the sun."

After breakfast we all wander down to the beach. Mum and Nana plop down on a sunbed straight away. Mum glugs sun-lotion thickly onto her legs which makes her look as if she's preparing to swim the English Channel.

Amy and I abandon the parents and wander over to the Dive Shack at the Carib Club. Jack tags along too. Why do little brothers always want to tag you wherever you go? At least Amy and Jack get on better these days.

We get there ten minutes early. Tristan and Katie-Louise have not arrived yet. We are greeted by a guy wearing flowery shorts and a Day-Glo T-shirt that says, '**The Carib Club says Live the Life**'.

"Hi you guys," he shouts in an American accent. "Come and join in the fun. My name's Guy and I'm here to make sure you all have a great holiday. Let me introduce you to Debbie, my best girl. She's the best when it comes to aerobics and dancing," he says, pointing to a very pretty girl next to him. She looks so cool in a tiny white bikini and gold shiny trainers.

Debbie and Guy

"Hi guys, you look like fun-lovers. What do you like to do best?" says Debbie as she flicks her long, dark hair over her shoulder.

"We're here to meet Tristan and Katie-Louise," I say, "They've booked a scuba -dive today." Just then Tristan and Katie-Louise arrive with two others.

"Hi!" says Tristan, "this is Marcus, our dive instructor, and this is Jenny, his assistant and dive buddy." Marcus is tall with brown floppy hair. Jenny only reaches his shoulder and wears her hair in two cute bunches. Marcus holds up his hand to high-five us all.

"Hi!" I return Marcus's high-five and do the same to Jenny. She beams a warm friendly smile revealing a large gap between her two front teeth.

"Do you have your P.A.D.I. qualifications?" asks Marcus.

"No we aren't qualified divers yet but Katie-Louise says it may be okay to do a try-dive." I say hopefully. "We have dived before in Canario Bonito though."

"We just need to make sure you can clear your masks underwater and go through the safety rules with you," says Marcus. "I'm afraid the little fellow is too young," Marcus points to Jack, "but with his parents' permission he can come on the boat with us and do some snorkelling. Jenny will stay with him."

"Sure! That's great," I say, answering for all of us. So exciting!

Jenny takes us to the equipment room. Amy and I kit up and Jack grabs a mask and snorkel. I'm familiar with the routine and the gear now as we've had lots of practise in Canario Bonito where we helped save the dolphins. Amy and I jump into the pool in our diving gear and Marcus gives us a revision lesson on breathing through the regulator and clearing our masks if they fill with water. Jack messes around in the shallow end to practise swimming with his mask and snorkel.

"Excellent!" says Marcus as we get out of the pool. "You have passed your training session." Jenny hands us some permission forms for our parents to complete.

"See you all back here at two o'clock for the dive," says Jenny.

The Cheeky Kid

"You all look like you've had a good morning," Mum says as Amy, Jack and I approach the parents' sun-beds. Mum still looks white and greasy. Dad is turning a reddish-pink colour.

"Oh Mum, it's great!" I yell. "We can go scuba-diving this afternoon if you give your permission."

"And I can go on the boat and do some snorkelling," yells Jack.

"Whoa! Hold on! You are so excited and speaking so quickly I can hardly understand you," Mum laughs. She reaches for a pen from her beach bag. Mum always has a pen handy. She scribbles her name on the permission forms. "Very good, it sounds great. Now let's go and have some lunch."

Suddenly, Dad yells out loud. "OUCH! What was that?"

"Ow! Something's just hit me," cries Mum. I look around and see a tangerine hurtling through the air. It whacks Dad's head. The missiles are coming from the direction of the little wooden houses close to the beach.

"I don't believe it!" yells Dad, "some little toe-rag is chucking tangerines at us from over there! Hey! Get out o' there you. . ." Another squashy tangerine hits Dad's head. His face turns luminous-orange as the juice drips down from his head.

"YOU!" cries Mum at the top of her voice, "WHAT DO YOU THINK YOU'RE PLAYING AT?" Just then a small boy with a cheeky face and a wide, grinning mouth bounds out from behind a house built on stilts. Dark curls peep out from under a red, green, yellow and black beanie hat.

"I'm playing 'Tango the Tourist', do you wan' a go?" replies the cheeky boy.

"No, we certainly don't!" I say. But then I remember my manners. "My name's Lottie, what's your name?" I hold out my hand ready to shake his politely.

The boy clasps my hand, locking fingers, and then switches to a hand-shake before finally banging his knuckles against mine in a fist thump. "This is the official Wadadidili greeting. I'm Charley Marley."

"What a funny name. Are you related to Bob Marley?" I hold back a giggle.

"I think I must be. I've got wicked rhythm, watch this." He does the funniest dance, EVER! Everyone laughs, even Dad with tangerine juice dripping down his face.

Charley Marley

"That's enough Charley Marley, it's making my tummy hurt," says Jack.

"I'm Jack. Do you live in that cool house?" Jack holds out his hand and Charley repeats his special handshake with him.

"Yeah, with my Granny Marley," he points to an old lady seated under a palm tree. She is selling bananas to a couple of tourists. "Yeah, come over and say hi."

"We'll leave you to it," says Dad. "I'm so hungry I could even eat those squashy tangerines." Dad and Mum set off to the restaurant for lunch and I go along with Jack, Amy and Charley to meet Granny Marley.

The old lady is sitting on an old banana crate covered with a red, green, yellow and black knitted blanket. Charley's beanie hat must have been made from the leftover wool. Granny Marley is wearing a blue striped blouse and a red spotted skirt and tied around her mop of curly hair is a red cotton scarf. She is grinning the same way as Charley, flashing her white teeth.

"Come with us after lunch, Charley," says Jack. "I'm allowed to go on the dive boat with Lottie and the others if your Granny allows you to."

"You can have all the bananas you can eat if you take Charley off my hands," she says with a deep-throated chuckle.

"Yeah, that'll be better than playing Tango the Tourists. Can I go Granny?"

"Yeah, as long as you don't go near Turtle Island," says Granny Marley.

I wonder what that is all about. Granny Marley keeps on talking. "I know there is bad voodoo on that island because I know the person causing it very well."

"Voodoo! Oh, that sounds spooky," says Amy.

"I will tell you about it." Granny Marley smiles at Amy in a kind way. "Her name is Het Scarrow and she was my best childhood friend. She was known as Hetty back then. We used to play on the beach together and wander around hand in hand. Life was very simple then, before the hotel was built and the tourists arrived. All the villagers used to grow their own food and keep animals outside their houses. We had pigs, cows and hens all running around outside. My Papa made us a swing in that very tree over there and we would take it in turns to push each other high in the sky."

"This is all very interesting Granny Marley" I bounce about from foot to foot and my tummy is rumbling like mad.

". . . Anyhow as I was saying," Granny Marley continues her ramblings. Amy's eyes are locked on hers and she is twiddling that straggly piece of hair at the back of her neck. "Something changed in her. We were both around twelve years of age and the hotel was built on our land by a rich man. At the time we had both been in trouble for fooling around with voodoo. We became interested in voodoo at school when some of the big girls brought in spells from the old families. Our mammas found out about the experiments and were very angry and frightened. We were not allowed out of the house for a whole week. They said we weren't to dabble in the voodoo because we might bring the bad luck to the house."

"So did you stop err . . . dabbling?" asks Amy.

"I did for a while but I decided I still wanted to learn more as it felt so right. Momma realized that I wouldn't give up so she took me to an old woman in the next village whose name was Eliza Kinty. Momma said if I was to learn about voodoo I must learn from a good voodoo witch. Eliza Kinty knew more about the craft than anyone else on the island. She taught me voodoo in a good way and how to use its powers against the wicked voodoo. Eliza was the Mother of Brightness and I visited her for many years while she transferred her knowledge to me.

"So what about this Hetty?" asks Amy, "What happened to her?"

"When Hetty and I reached the age of twenty-one I had a weird feeling about her. A Scottish man came to stay at the hotel and began talking to her on the beach. You may have met him. He owns the hotel now. After that I saw less and less of her and she became distant and strange. Some people say she was dabbling with the wicked voodoo."

"Yes. We met the owner at the welcome party. Hamish MacDougal," I say. "But what's he to do with Turtle Island?"

"If they are on Turtle Island I fear all is not well. Look over yonder," Granny Marley points at a huge bird waddling down the beach. "See that bird . . . that is the duppy bird. They are very rare and when you see one of those it is a very bad omen." I look down the beach to see the huge ground-dove spin around flashing its bright crimson eyes. "All is not well," says Granny Marley.

I think Granny Marley is nice but probably bonkers!

Duppy Bird

The Mystery of Turtle Island

I can't wait to get to the dive shack to pick up our equipment for the diving expedition. We help load the kit into the dive boat. The boat has *Fish 'n' Fins* painted on the side of it. The tanks are really heavy. Marcus and Jenny, the dive instructors, help to lift them into the boat and fasten them safely under the seats. Debbie stands around. I expect she can't risk breaking a glittery fingernail. We all climb onto the boat. Debbie plonks on a bench and puts her feet up. Amy and I squeeze onto a small wooden bench seat at the back. Guy shows up at the last minute, so Debbie has to make a space for him by putting her feet down. Good!

"All aboard!" shouts Leroy the captain, "Marcus is going to give you all a quick briefing then we can have an afternoon of sea and fun." Leroy starts the boat's engine and we are off. Tristan stands next to him as he is learning how to boat-handle. The sea is calm and still as we zoom along. Wadadidili beach is soon a tiny white strip in the distance. The boat passes another island in the distance. This one looks like a giant turtle.

"Is that Turtle Island?" I ask Charley.

"Yeah! My Granny will go mad if she finds out we are going anywhere near it."

"Have you been to Turtle Island before, Charley?" asks Jack.

"No, and if Granny Marley had known we were coming close to here she would not have allowed me to come," Charley replies seriously.

"Why not?" I ask.

"No one goes there, ever, because of the wicked voodoo witch, Het Scarrow," he says with a shudder.

"Mumbo-jumbo," says Jack, "who's Het Scarrow then?"

"Did you not listen to Granny Marley? She's a voodoo witch who turns children into Picos," says Charley as he makes witchy signs with his fingers.

"What are Picos?" Amy asks.

"Picos are creatures that look like Picasso made them," replies Charley.

"You mean Picasso the artist who painted eyes in the wrong places and people's bottoms at the front instead of at the back?" asks Jack.

"Exactly! These creatures were once children like us but have been changed so all their bodies are twisted. Some have two noses, some have eyes in the wrong places and most have their feet on back to front. They all have spiky hair styles in different colours like electric blue, vivid violet, luminous yellow and acidic green. My Granny Marley will go nuts if she knows we are going anywhere near Het Scarrow," says Charley.

"You are joking, right?" Amy is now looking worried. She can be a bit of a wimp at times. She's so gullible.

"Oh, take no notice, Amy; he's just trying to spook us," I reassure her, "Anyway look! We are going past it. It looks so pretty though. Look at that gorgeous white beach over there. I hope that's where we can have a rest and explore later." I point to a palm-lined beach which looks awesome. The boat slows down and Leroy plops the anchor in to the deep, indigo sea.

"Everybody ready?" asks Marcus, standing at the bow of the boat. "Safety first! Snorkellers, put on your life-jackets. Divers, kit up! Blow some air in to your buoyancy control jackets then do a buddy check before we get in the water." Amy and I attach our regulators to the tanks and test them. The compressed air whooshes out making a hissing sound. This means the equipment is working properly.

Guy stands at the bow of the boat with Marcus. "Now remember to always keep your partner and the dive leader Marcus in sight. I shall remain on the boat with Debbie and Captain Leroy. Jenny will take the snorkellers to the shallower water close to the beach."

We take turns to leap from the boat and follow Marcus down and down into the deep water. I love this feeling of weightlessness. It's like being an astronaut in space. I can do somersaults, flipping over and over through the water. Shoals of colourful fish swim up to my mask to check me out. *'Why have you invaded our world?'* They seem to ask. The water is so clear I can see the sea-bed below. I spot a jelly-fish. Eeek! I'm scared of jelly-fish. It drifts away from me. Good!

Marcus does the O.K. sign with his finger and thumb making an "O" shape. We each return the sign. Then he points above. A dark shape appears overhead blocking out the brightness of the sun's rays for a second. I feel a weird flip in my tummy then an explosion of delight. A turtle is swimming above me. It glides on through the water by the slow flailing movement of its giant front flippers. Wow! It opens its mouth wide and gobbles up the nasty jelly-fish. I didn't know turtles ate jelly-fish. I watch it glide away into the wide, wide sea.

With the nasty jelly-fish out of the way I glide along too, gazing at corals the colour of precious jewels. I'd remembered not to touch coral. It's a living organism and touching would kill it. Suddenly a large moray eel pops his head out of a crevice in the rock and makes me jump. My eyes lock onto its large teeth. I don't want to touch that at all!

All too soon the dive is over. We follow Marcus back to the *Fish 'n' Fins* dive boat.

I spit the regulator out of my mouth as soon as we surface. "That was absolutely brilliant!" I say.

"You all did really well," says Marcus, "I'll be happy to take you to Barracuda Reef tomorrow if you like."

"Oh, yes please!" we all yell at once.

Once we are back on the boat we take off the scuba gear and store it under the seats. Leroy allows Tristan to drive the boat to shore. Jack and Charley are already running around on the beach.

"What was it like, Lottie?" Jack asks, "The snorkelling is just awesome! We saw lots of little fishes."

"Like floating in a different universe!" I say, "It's like being part of the underwater world. I felt like a mermaid and could have stayed there forever! What are you eating?"

"Banana and papaya," says Charley, "Granny Marley put them in the boat for us. Want some?"

"Yes please, I'm starving."

It's lovely sitting on the beach with my best friend Amy. I put my arm around her as we both just sit quietly for a while, staring out to sea.

"Do you think Turtle Island is haunted by a voodoo witch, Lottie?" Amy asks.

"No way! It's all made up, as Jack says," I reply. "There are *real* things to worry about other than silly rumours."

Just then Leroy shouts, "All aboard!"

We wade through the shallow warm water to board the *Fish 'n' Fins* for the sail back to the Royal Wadadidili Hotel.

As I bounce from side to side, perched on the seats of the boat, I see something in the distance. At first I think it is another island. But I'm wrong. As the boat sails closer I let out a little gasp. It's a horrible floating mass of plastic waste. Objects cast aside by thoughtless humans. An island of plastic water bottles, babies' nappies, shampoo bottles, six-pack holders, straws and a totally disgusting rainbow of bottle tops.

Then I spot it. Something is moving in the middle of all this garbage.

Plastic Island

Leroy drives the boat close to the plastic island. In the middle of all this stinky rubbish is . . .

A turtle!

"Look!" I point at the turtle. He is thrashing around among all the plastic bottles and rubbish. I'd seen something on TV about this. *Blue Planet* is my favourite programme and there was an episode about the harm that plastic is doing to our oceans and sea-creatures. This is different though. I'm seeing it for myself. Real, horrible plastic waste! It's spoiling this beautiful, clear blue sea.

"The little fellow is in deep trouble," yells Marcus. It's then I see what's wrong. The poor turtle has a plastic, drinking straw stuck up his nostril. He must be struggling to breathe properly.

Poor Little Turtle!

"We must do something," I cry.

"Let's not panic him!" says Tristan.

"I can't believe it!" cries Katie-Louise. "Leroy, get the boat as close as you can. We must rescue it." Leroy cuts the engine and steers the *Fish 'n' Fins* through the dirty plastic until we reach the turtle. Tristan pulls on his mask and jumps over the side, splashing into the sea of plastic.

Quickly I slip on my mask and snorkel and . . . Splash! I take a giant leap into the water to help him. Straight under the bobbing rubbish I go. I open my eyes and look up to the surface. I'm drowning in plastic! It's dark and scary. The sunlight can hardly penetrate. My plastic snorkel pushes its way through all the dirty litter. Bobbing above my head I see coffee cup lids, a toy dinosaur, a yogurt pot, a cheap plastic rain coat, a flip-flop and a pair of plastic headphones. I take a deep breath through my snorkel and push my head through the disgusting junk. As my head pokes through, a chunk of cling-film wraps around my mad curls and the plastic headphones dangle around my neck. I must look like the monster from the Black Lagoon! No time to worry about my looks now. We need to lift this baby turtle onto the boat.

He's quite heavy and seems scared to bits. I'm not surprised. I'd be frightened if I had a drinking straw stuck up my nose and had to swim through that load of trash. We yank him up onto the diving platform at the back of the boat. Katie-Louise already has the first aid kit open. She rubs her hand gently over his shell and checks underneath.

"He's an adult male and probably weighs around thirty-five kilos. I would take him to the sea-life specialist centre but I think I can remove the straw myself and cause him less stress," Katie-Louise says as she takes a pair of metal tweezers out of the box. Here's the bit where I want to turn my head. "Hold his head still, Lottie," she says. I have no choice. I have to watch.

Katie-Louise grabs the end of the straw with the tweezers. She wiggles it gently back and forth. Oh no, poor turtle. Bright scarlet blood oozes from his nostril. I feel queasy. The turtle is wiggling like mad and I have a job on keeping his head still.

"Soon be over little one," I whisper to him. My gentle words seem to calm him for a moment. Then I see the straw slowly emerging out of his nostril. It's caked in gunk and blood but the turtle is free. Katie-Louise puts the straw in the rubbish bin on the boat.

"We must recycle that nasty thing properly when we get to shore. The thing is with plastic straws not every re-cycle centre will take them. They have to be collected and shipped to a specialist centre in America," she says. "Leroy, take the boat away from this horrible mess and we'll let the turtle go free. Leroy starts the engine. I'm glad to get away from the revolting mess. When we are in the clear water, Katie-Louise attaches a small tag to the turtle's fin.

"I will call this one Timmy," she says as she writes something in a notebook. She then gently eases Timmy off the dive platform and he splashes into the clean sea.

I watch as the turtle swims away from the boat. Yippee! We have saved Timmy. Now, what can be done about the plastic waste?

"I hate all that plastic in the sea," I say to no one in particular.

"It's a massive problem," says Tristan.

"Yes, our planet is being destroyed by plastic waste," says Katie-Louise. "During my spare time I work for a cosmetic company called *Tropic*. I am an ambassador and we have lots of meetings to discuss how the cosmetic companies can help to reduce the pollution."

"Yeah! I noticed that most of the plastic bottles floating in that mess are shampoo, conditioners, face creams and stuff like that," I say.

"Yes and some things are so very tiny you can't see them," says Katie-Louise, "such as micro-beads that are used in face scrubs and toothpaste. They cause so much harm to sea-life."

We are drowning in plastic. What can we do? I bite the inside of my cheek as I think about this horrible issue.

Turtle Watch

It had been an exciting but traumatic afternoon. On our way back to the Wadadidili Hotel, Katie-Louise tells us about the work she is doing at Plymouth University.

"The marine biology course is awesome," Katie-Louise says. "There's a lot of theory and research to get through but the best bit is the practical work. I couldn't believe my luck when I was assigned this turtle project here in the Caribbean."

"What's the turtle project about?" Amy asks.

"The project is about why the loggerhead turtle population is rapidly in decline on this island. We are tagging turtles so we can trace their whereabouts. Hey! I'm on Turtle Watch tonight. Would you like to come?"

"Wow!" I can't believe my luck. "You betcha!" I yell. Now I need to ask the parents about an extended bedtime.

* * *

Negotiating with the parents was easy-peasy. Mum and Dad are always in a good mood on holiday. I'm so excited!

High tide is at three minutes past midnight. The only other time I'd stayed up after midnight was New Year's Eve and when we all saved the dolphins in Canario Bonito last half term. We sit quietly in a sandy place underneath the coconut trees. A half-moon peeks through the clouds. The soft sound of the sea creates a hushed magical atmosphere.

Then I spot it! A turtle! I've seen three turtles in one day. This was a huge, adult turtle."Look! I can see one!" I cry as I turn to Katie-Louise.

"Hush!" Katie-Louise whispers, "It's a loggerhead turtle. Any noise or disturbance during nesting could cause the mother turtle to panic and return to the water without covering her eggs." I keep as still as a statue. I don't want the turtle to be scared of us.

As the wave crests the loggerhead turtle slides onto the beach and pauses in the sea foam to look around. She is about a metre in length. "Wow!" I whisper.

"She's been migrating at sea for over two years and is returning to a spot within fifty yards of where she had made her last nest," Katie-Louise whispers in my ear. Slowly, the turtle begins to crawl, a slow, awkward, unnatural movement for her. As she works very hard, pulling with her front flippers and pushing with more power with her rear legs, she pauses frequently to study the beach. "She's stopping to look for dry land and for danger, for a predator or any unusual movement," Katie-Louise whispers. I keep still so she doesn't spot me. I hope Amy is doing the same.

The turtle inches forward towards us leaving a wobbly trail in the sand. Then she stops. She is very close to us and about thirty metres from the sea. She's found her spot and begins flinging away loose sand with her front flippers, using her cupped rear flippers as shovels.

"She's now forming the body pit," whispers Katie-Louise. I can see a round shallow burrow about ten centimetres deep. As she digs she rolls her body to even the indentation. This reminds me of Dad making sandcastles and spaceships in the sand with Jack. "For a creature of the water, it is tedious work and she pauses often to rest." When the body pit is finished she begins digging even deeper. "She's now constructing the egg cavity," says Katie-Louise. I can just make out a teardrop-shaped chamber.

The huge turtle finishes her work and rests some more. Then slowly she covers the egg cavity with the rear of her body. Then something awesome happens. Three eggs drop at the same time, each shell covered with some yucky stuff. They are too soft and flexible to break as they plop into the sand. More eggs follow, two and three at a time. While she lays the eggs she doesn't move. "Can you see her tears?" Katie-Louise whispers in my ear. "Turtles seem to cry as they lay their eggs." I smile when I see the shining salty stream trickle from her droopy eyes. "They cry all the time to regulate salt, but laying eggs is often the only time they're observed on land."

I keep so still and hold my breath. The laying continues without interruption.

"When the clutch holds a hundred eggs, the turtle is finished for the night and begins covering them with sand," Katie-Louise explains. "When the cavity is filled, she packs the sand and uses her front flippers to refill the body pit and disguise the nest. When she begins moving I know the nesting is over and the eggs are safe."

We all keep as still as statues and gaze as the turtle carefully spreads sand over her nest and scatters it in all directions to fool any predators. What a clever turtle! Satisfied her nest is safe; the turtle begins her cumbersome-cumbersome crawl back to the water, leaving behind the eggs.

"What happens to the eggs now?" Amy whispers.

"She will never bother with them again," Katie-Louise replies. "She will repeat the nesting once or twice during the season before migrating back to her feeding ground, hundreds of miles away. In a year or two, maybe three or four, she will return to the same beach and nest again."

"Imagine going through all that and never seeing your kids EVER!" I say.

"Now *The Turtle Watch* volunteers will come along soon and do their work. They are fighting fiercely to protect the nests. We have to tell off the tourists for tampering with the protected areas. The law is on our side," Katie-Louise explains.

"So what happens to the clutch of eggs now?" Amy asks.

"In sixty days or so, depending on the temperature of the sand, the hatchlings will come to life. With no help from their mother, they will crack open their shells and dig out in a group effort that could take days," Katie-Louise explains. "When the time is right, usually at night or in a rainstorm when the temperature is cooler, they will make a run for it. Together they will burst from the cavity, take a second to get oriented, then hustle down to the water and swim away. The odds are stacked against them. The ocean is a minefield with so many predators. Come on, you two. I'd better get you back to the hotel. "

As we walk away, we carefully kick sand over the turtle's tracks to make them disappear. What a night!

Beach Investigation

Tossing and turning in my bed, I just can't sleep! Everything has been so exciting and I can't stop thinking about those teeny-weeny turtle eggs.

Turtle Island is intriguing too. My brain is still buzzing and fizzing. I tap onto Google to search. A map of Turtle Island pops up. Turtle Island is small compared to Wadadidili Island. I bet I could walk from one side to the other in less than an hour. Climbing those hills would be tough though. Anyone would need a small boat to get across the huge Wobblite Lake too. The lake seems to flow out into the sea at Turtle Bay. Turtle Bay is tiny and looks to be only accessible by boat. Sandy Bay is the white sandy beach where the snorkellers swam in the shallow water. Steep rocks surround the whole island. The weird thing is Turtle Island is actually shaped like a turtle. This reminds me of the turtle laying her eggs tonight.

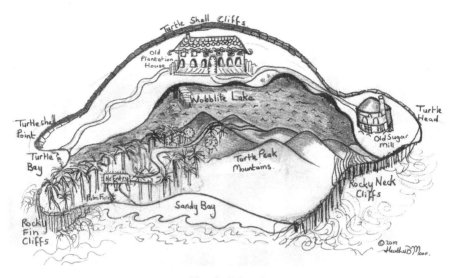

Turtle Island

I know it's naughty but I need to check that the turtle eggs are safe. Amy is doing one of her snoring routines. Sneaking out of bed, I tip-toe across the floor and gently open the hotel room door. The parents are fast asleep. I can hear their snores. It's like *Britain's Got Talent Snoring Contest* in here. I won't be missed. I sneak down to the beach again. Then I see something weird.

Two figures are approaching from a boat at the shoreline. They stop when they see the turtle tracks, and then slowly follow them to the nest. We mustn't have done a great job when trying to disguise the tracks. They are studying the site with flashlights. I can hear their soft voices but I am safely hidden from their view behind a palm tree.

Maybe it's only the Turtle Watch team. I take a good look at the boat and make a mental note of the name painted on the side. *Highlander.*

* * *

First thing the next morning, I decide I need to check out the turtle nest. Over breakfast, I tell Amy about last night. She thinks I'm crazy leaving a warm cosy bed to investigate a turtle nest. A good detective must do risky things!

"Come on, Amy," I grab her hand and run down to the beach to where the turtle nest is. When we get there I see a wire fence has been constructed to secure the crevice where the turtle has laid her eggs. A sign says;

Caution! Turtle eggs! Do not enter

"The Turtle Watch must have been here early," says Amy.

Satisfied that the turtle eggs will be safely buried until the hatchlings appear, Amy and I go to the Dive Shack to prepare for our dive to Barracuda Reef today. Jack and Charley aren't allowed to join us as the water is too deep and there is no beach to snorkel. Great! It's just me, Amy, Katie-Louise and Tristan diving with Marcus and Jenny today. I like Jenny; she's not as much of a show off as that Debbie girl. Guy isn't with us either. They *have some important work to do*. Good! He's a bit of a creep anyway!

The diving at Barracuda Reef is brilliant. We see lots of barracuda. I am a bit scared of them at first. They have scary expressions on their faces and are huge. They look like silver sharks and seem to glare at me with spooky eyes as they glide past. Amy is doing really well. I thought she would have freaked out by now.

On our way back to the hotel we pass Turtle Island. I glance over towards the lovely, white sandy beach and wish we could stop there again. I spot a lovely old sugar plantation nestled in the hillside. I would love to go exploring but Marcus says there's a storm forecast for later and he does not want to risk getting caught in it. Leroy whizzes us back to Royal Wadadidili Hotel in the boat.

Back at the hotel I notice that the sky on the horizon is changing colour from a deep blue to a murky purple. It seems a storm is gathering in the far distance. Marcus was right not to stay out at sea any longer. I'm glad to be back at the resort and ready for some lunch.

Before we can eat, we have to rinse all the scuba gear off in freshwater. It's a bit of a drag, washing the salt water off the equipment but Marcus has explained it is essential to do this. Salt water causes damage to the kit. I suppose it would be even more of a drag if we were thirty meters down in the ocean's depths and something went wrong with the equipment!

Amy and I stroll back along the beach to the hotel restaurant for lunch. We wander past the crevice where the turtle had laid her eggs. Something does not feel right. The sand has been disturbed and scattered around. "I hope the turtle eggs are safe," I say to Amy.

"It's probably a stray dog digging around," Amy says. I notice a swirly pattern imprinted in the sand. I've seen this design before somewhere . . . but where? I get up close and snap a photo with my flashy new phone and I then snap a second pic of where it is in relation to the turtle nest. A good detective needs to gather information at any time . . . just in case!

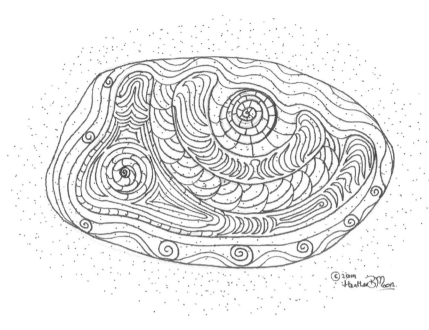

A Swirly Pattern in the Sand

"I'll mention it to Katie-Louise when I see her," I say.

I glance out to sea. I can see Jack and Charley playing on a blue plastic sea-tractor. Laughter and giggles drift across on the breeze. I give them a wave and they wave back at us.

"Are you coming in for some lunch now Jack?" I yell. He's either ignoring me or can't hear. Jack has selective hearing when he's having fun. He'll come in when he's hungry. "Don't be long now. There's a tropical storm gathering."

Lunch is delicious. I choose a fresh tuna salad and Amy has a chicken burger. Mum and Dad are sitting with Nana and Pop at another table so we let them continue their adult conversation in peace.

Suddenly, just as I'm about to take a bite of tuna salad there is a mighty *CRACK!*

BOOM!

51

CRACK!
BOOM!
FLASH!

I leap up and rush to the window. Thunder rumbles. Lightning flashes, lighting up the sky like sparkling fireworks. The tropical storm is here. Everyone has abandoned the beach, even the jet-ski attendants. But where is Jack? Better not panic the parents just yet.

Tropical Storm

I dash down to the beach with Amy in close pursuit. Rain is now hammering down like a waterfall. Mad hair is sticking to my face like glue. No sign of Jack and Charley or the sea-tractor. The other sea-tractors have been lifted high up onto the sand but the blue one is missing. So where are Jack and Charley? Maybe they are sheltering with Granny Marley until the storm is over. I see Granny Marley's face peeping through the window of her tiny house on stilts.

"Hi, Granny Marley," I say. It doesn't feel right calling her Granny, she's not my grandma.

"Hello, girls! Quick! Come inside into the dry."

"We thought Charley and Jack may be here with you," I say.

"Oh! I thought they may be with you, taking shelter in the hotel." Deep wrinkles form on her forehead as she glances through the window.

"They were playing on the blue sea-tractor but it's disappeared," says Amy.

"We'd better go and find out where the boys are," I say. "We'll be back when we have some news. Try not to worry, Granny Marley."

"I hope they haven't been blown over to Turtle Island on that silly sea-tractor," Granny Marley says. Now I'm worried too. I want to hurry off to find Jack and Charley.

"Come on, Amy! No time to waste." Getting the parents involved isn't an option. It will waste even more time. If Amy and I can find

Jack and Charley on our own it will save them getting into trouble too. The parents will make so much fuss.

The rain is still hammering down and the sea is like a boiling witch's cauldron. I spot the jet-skis on the beach. A naughty plan begins to fizz in my head. Boy, will I be in deep trouble if we do this but if we can find the boys and pull them back to shore on their sea-tractor with a jet-ski it will be all over before the parents have finished their puddings. There is no sign of the attendant with the gold tooth.

"Quick Amy! Help me get this into the sea and jump on the back."

"No way!" She is rubbing her arms as though it's freezing cold.

"Amy, I said quickly! This is not the time for one of your wimpy moments." She knows when I mean business and I'm spared the whimpering about wicked voodoo, rough sea and getting ourselves into deep trouble. As soon as she gets her leg over the double seat I grip the control lever and BROOM! BROOM! We're off.

We bounce up and down, the waves whizzing and whooshing from side to side, heading further out to sea. There is no sign of the blue sea-tractor anywhere.

"We're heading for Turtle Island!" Amy yells. She says something else but it's lost in the wind.

As we approach the sandy beach of Turtle Island I can see something blue. I drive the jet-ski close to the shoreline. Oh no! It's as I feared. The blue thing I see is the plastic sea-tractor . . . and it's smashed to bits!

The Man-Beast

I drive the jet-ski up onto the beach as I've watched the beach attendants do. We both get off and look around. I kick at the washed up plastic waste and rubbish.

"What do we do now?" Amy asks.

"Well, I'm pretty sure Jack and Charley made it here." Now I'm wishing I'd not acted so quickly. Maybe I should have informed the parents. They will be missing us now and worrying like parents do.

"Call them on your flashy phone," says Amy. I take the phone out of the zipped-up pocket of my shorts. No signal and I think it's got too wet!

"Come on, Amy," I say, "we will just have to look around and search for the boys." I walk to the end of the beach. The rain seems to be easing off a bit although the wind makes spooky howling sounds through the branches of the palm trees. I begin to climb the steep path at the end of the beach. It leads to a forest of palm trees and rainbow-coloured bushes. Amy is following behind, twisting and turning her head around as she walks. Broken bits of coconut shells crunch under my flip-flops as I walk. Then I come to a rope strung across the path. There is a sign which says:

DANGER! NO ENTRY!

"What do we do now?" Amy asks. "Shall we turn back?"

"No chance!" I say. "Look!" I point to something on the path ahead. It's soggy and covered in sand but I know exactly what it is. "Look! It's Charley's beanie hat!" I yell above the wind. "They definitely came this way!"

"Yeah!" says Amy. "Unless someone stole his hat and turned them into Picos."

"Amy, you are a wet-wipe!" I say. "How can you believe in such nonsense? Come on!" I duck under the rope and race to pick up the hat.

"Lottie, I think I saw something move near that tree just now." Amy points to a tree covered in red flowers. "I saw an animal with spiky horns."

"Don't be silly, Amy. Your imagination is getting the better of you." I say. Her face is the colour of pale custard. "Come on, I thought you'd stopped being a wimp after our adventures in Europe when we saved the bees.

"I'm not being a wimp, Lottie. I definitely saw something move."

Suddenly the branches of the tree rustle and out bounds the scariest thing I have seen EVER!

It's A BEAST-MONSTER!

The gigantic beast-monster plods towards me. EEEK! As the beast-monster gets closer I can see he has the right leg of a beast and a left leg of a human. Or, at least, there is a Nike trainer shoe on the left foot. The beast-monster is covered in brown fur and has pointy horns protruding from his head. My dad used to read a book to me when I was a little kid. The beast-monster reminds me of the creature in the book but this is scarier in real life.

"It's got big horns!" whispers Amy. "I told you there was something watching us from behind a tree." I notice it has a huge hairy hoof at the end of its right leg. Its head is covered in spiky fur.

"HELLO THERE!" booms the voice of the weird beast-monster. I almost jump out of my flip-flops.

EEEK! Hairy-scary!

56

Papa Zakarus

Then he speaks to us again. "I've come to see if you're alright," the beast-monster says. Now I wasn't expecting that! "Let me introduce myself. I am Papa Zakarus, keeper of the forest. I am protector of birds and beasts. Meet Choppa my companion."

A beautiful hummingbird, I had not noticed before, flew down from the horn on his head and hovered in front of us. "He likes you," says Papa Zakarus, his face crinkling into a smile. "Now meet Izzy-Lizzy my iguana friend, he seems to like you too." This is not what I expected. Totally bizarre! I glance down at my feet. A ginormous iguana is licking my foot with its long tongue. Eeek! I look up at Papa Zakarus.

"My little brother and his friend Charley Marley have been ship-wrecked . . . well more like tractor-wrecked," I say.

"Charley Marley, I know that name. He must belong to the Marley family of Wadadidili. I know the family they are good people," says Papa Zakarus. "Sit down on this rock while I tell you about the island and its dangers." We both plonk down as we are told. My shorts are still wet anyway. There is something kind about this big, gentle half-man. He is wearing a pair of tatty yellow shorts and his hairy hands have long claws at the end of each finger. He has kind, human eyes which twinkle brightly as he speaks to us.

Papa Zakarus: His First Story

Papa Zakarus reaches into the pocket of his tatty shorts with his clawed-hands and pulls out a pendant. Papa Zakarus holds out the pendant for us to see. It is made of glistening gold and is divided into two parts. The top part has a round space which has the image of a white wolf in the centre. The wolf-image seems to move, as though it is alive. He begins to tell us a story in his gentle voice.

The Sacred Pendant

"Long, long ago, way back in time, there lived the ancient tribes of the Aardvark Indians. One Indian tribe occupied two beautiful islands, Wadadidili and Turtle Island. A young boy named Aaron von Dyke belonged to this tribe. One day he was hunting in the forest to feed his

60

family with his faithful wolf cub, Aztilum. As he stood by a Tamarind tree he aimed his spearhead in the direction of a fat, juicy rat gnawing on the carcass of a dead bird.

"Suddenly a whoosh of searing heat launched the rat across the sizzling moss on the ground. Aaron jumped back in terror. The Tamarind tree had exploded into a torrent of flames. Swirling, whirly clouds of smoke rose from the blaze making Aaron's eyes water and causing Aztilum to sneeze wolf juices into the air. As the atmosphere began to clear, his blurry eyes locked onto a vision of stunning beauty. The bright spirit of goodness, Voodoodia appeared before them.

"She began to speak to them in a voice softer than fluffy angel-hair. 'Aaron von Dyke and Aztilum, do not be afraid of me. You are both good beings. The Voodoolites have chosen you to carry their goodness to these Caribbean islands,' she said. 'Take this Sacred Pendant, you must guard it with your lives and protect it from reaching evil hands. The Koracky-Nimo diamond, which is set within the pendant, has great power as it is mined from a spiritual place under the bed of the sea. You must hand this down to your children Aaron von Dyke. Aztilum, when your life is over, your wolf powers will become great and your spirit will inhabit the Sacred Pendant for all time.'"

Papa Zakarus moves the pendant closer to us and says, "This is the Sacred Pendant of Wadadidili and Turtle Island. I was collecting breadfruit from a tree one day when Izzy-Lizzy dug it out of the ground when she scratched for grubs to eat. I have since discovered its powers. The wolf you see in the centre of the pendant is Aztilum who is a powerful wolf spirit. He has a magnificent sense of smell and uses the magnetic force of these sacred feathers to search for things." Papa Zakarus points to the silver feathers which are attached to the pendant. Attached to the top part, by a blue bead, hangs a smaller circular piece with a hole in the middle.

"As you can see, there is a large jewel missing from here." Papa Zakarus points to the hole in the golden metal of the lower pendant which is surrounded by more blue beads.

"What kind of jewel is missing?" I ask.

"It is the very powerful and valuable Korecky-Nimo diamond which was stolen by a bad woman called Het Scarrow. She stole it from me to give her more power in her practice of wicked voodoo," says Papa Zakarus, "I have been trying to find it for years but she has hidden it well. This is one of the reasons I stay here."

"So Charley was right," says Amy, "Het Scarrow is a real person . . . a wicked voodoo witch. Does she really turn children into Picos then?"

"Oh yes, she does indeed," Papa Zakarus continues. "If children have wandered away from their parents while visiting the island or if they have gone too far out to sea the Ru-B-Loos capture them and take them to Het Scarrow."

"What are Ru-B-Loos?" Amy asks.

"Ru-B-Loos are Het Scarrow's assistants. They are disguised as beautiful young fashion girls so that the children are not frightened of them. They can then approach the children to lure them away. They sing songs and lullabies to the children to hypnotize them to sleep. Once the children are in deep slumber Het Scarrow casts her voodoo spells on the children and turns them into Picos."

"Ugh! That's horrible," says Amy. "So even if we find Jack and Charley the Ru-B-Roos may have captured them and they could be Picos by now!"

Amy is so gullible, I think to myself again.

"It could be possible. They watch the coast for anyone in difficulty and then take them to a secret place," says Papa Zakarus.

"Tell us more about the Ru-B-Loos," I say treating this half-man to my best eye roll. He's probably wearing some kind of fancy dress outfit left over from Halloween. There is no way I'm going to be captured by some cool fashion girl in high heels. *Mumbo-jumbo* as Jack would say!

"The Ru-B-Loos are really difficult to spot," Papa Zakarus continues to explain. "The only way to expose a Ru-B-Loo is to scatter rice on the ground close to them as they are then obligated to gather every grain. If they do that you know it is one of the creatures.

"You must act swiftly," says Papa Zakarus. "I'm sorry I can't come with you all the way. I'm not allowed to go beyond Wobblite Lake. Het Scarrow put a curse on me which I will tell you more about later when we know the boys are safe. Make your way through the forest while there is still a glimmer of sunlight to find your way. Take the Sacred Pendant, Aztilum will show you the way to the boys."

"How will he do that?" I ask, gazing at the image of the wolf in the pendant.

"Do you have anything that belongs to Charley or Jack so we can give Aztilum the scent to follow?" asks Papa Zakarus.

"I found this," I say, showing Papa Zakarus Charley's knitted beanie hat. I hand it to him and roll my eyes again. It's as though a long-dead wolf can sniff the scent a boy on a beanie hat. This is ridiculous!

Papa Zakarus holds the beanie hat close to the image of Aztilum in the centre of the Sacred Pendant. Once again the wolf-image seems to move. His nose tics and twitches. Then something weird happened. One of the silver feathers on the pendant flips up and points to the path ahead. No way!

"Aztilum is showing us the way!" I say jumping up and bouncing from foot to foot. I have no other choice. I'd better believe in this *mumbo-jumbo* for now. "Does this mean he thinks Charley and Jack have gone through the forest Papa Zakarus?"

"Indeed he does, there may be hope that the boys have survived the wild sea," Papa Zakarus replies."

"Yes, but will they survive Het Scarrow?" says Amy.

With that, we follow the path that leads through the scary forest.

Picos!

The path is slippery and my flip-flops are totally useless.

"We are coming to the lake soon," says Papa Zakarus, "You must collect some jelly-fish eggs."

"Ugh! Are there jelly-fish in the lake?" asks Amy, "If there are, I'm not going near it. They can give you a nasty sting you know."

"Yes, the lake is full of freshwater jelly-fish called Wobblites," Papa Zakarus replies. "Their sting is not as nasty as sea-water jelly-fish though, so no need to worry. They produce eggs called wobbits. I know for certain that Het Scarrow is allergic to wobbits because I once saw her swallow some by accident when she was swimming in the lake. An itchy rash broke out all over her body and she was violently sick."

The silver feathers point up the hill leading into the dark forest. Choppa leads the way, flying ahead as we climb the hill. As we get deeper and deeper into the forest the trees are spooky, staring with eerie eyes. Tiny pin-pricks shoot up and down my arms.

Just then I see a flicker of movement behind the dark, ghostly bushes where Choppa is hovering.

"Look! Papa Zakarus, what's that over there?" I ask, pointing to the bushes.

"Stay here. I'll have a look," he says. He plods over to the spot. Beaming his widest grin he waves at us with his clawed hand. "Come here and meet some of my friends." We both tiptoe towards him. Four of the strangest boys I've seen, EVER are hiding behind the bushes.

One boy has two eyes on the same side of his face. The second one has a nose where his ear should be. The third has only one eye but has two noses. The fourth has bendy arms and legs. All the boys have spiky, brightly-coloured hair and some of their bodies are twisted so that their feet and their bottoms are facing the wrong way. So it's true! Picos really do exist on Turtle Island. This is *so weird*.

Picos

"Meet my Pico friends, Robbie, Shaun, Kris and Jamie," says Papa Zakarus. The peculiar boys look scared to bits. They hold out their hands to fist-bump us.

"Hi, I'm Lottie," I fist-bump them each in turn.

"My friends were once normal children just like you until they were taken by the Ru-B-Loos. Het Scarrow cast her wicked spell on them and changed them into Picos," explains Papa Zakarus.

"Is there anything that can change them back again?" Amy asks.

"Only taking away Het's powers will undo the spell. That must be done by someone who has a greater power with the voodoo magic than her," Papa Zakarus replies.

"Who has a greater power than Het Scarrow though?" I ask.

Papa Zakarus stares at me with his sad human eyes, "It must be a witch who practises good voodoo."

"Do you know a good voodoo witch, Papa Zakarus?" I ask.

"Not on this island but I did once, long ago before . . ."

"Before what, Papa Zakarus?" Amy interrupts.

"Before I . . ." Papa Zakarus was about to tell us something but he stops.

Wobblite Lake

We have reached the end of the forest path. The silver feathers on the Sacred Pendant are doing their nut. Twitching and pointing towards the lake at the foot of the hill. Papa Zakarus points to the huge lake. "There it is, Wobblite Lake. Can you both swim?"

"Yes, we can. We are both scuba divers." I don't mention that I'm scared of jelly-fish as I put on my best brave-face.

"Do we have to swim in there?" Amy asks, making her wimpy face.

"Yes, we do!" I reply. "Our clothes are still wet anyway. Come on!" I wade in from the water's edge. The lake gets deeper and deeper until it's up to my waist. Then I feel something tickle my leg. Ugh! Through the clear water I can see zillions of jelly-fish around my legs. Long, slimy purple tentacles tickle my skin. Yuk! I hope they don't sting. Then, I see something sparkle out of the corner of my eye, but I can't be sure. "Come on, Amy, you can do it. They only tickle. Just . . ." Suddenly the lake bed drops away under my feet. The water is so deep I can't feel the bottom. There's no choice. I have to swim for it. I'm worried more about my new phone than the jelly-fish now. It'll be completely ruined!

Thankfully, Amy and Papa Zakarus are following me. We all manage to swim across the jelly-fish lake and drag ourselves out onto the dry land at the other side.

"Hurry now!" shouts Papa Zakarus, "I've collected enough Wobbits in my sack so you must go." I glance at the Sacred Pendant. "You must hurry girls and find Jack and Charley. I can't accompany you any further than this. Go now, before it's too late. Goodbye girls. I will pop the sack of Wobbits behind this tamarind tree. I'll still be here when you need me." He turns away from us and I suddenly feel sad and alone even though I have Amy.

The Ru-B-Loos

"We've no time to waste, Amy," I turn to my friend. "I'm beginning to believe this voodoo nonsense after all. We need to find Jack and Charley quickly." I spot an old wooden raft tied to a post at the side of the water's edge. Someone must use this old raft to get across this lake. Sure enough the silver feathers twitch as I hold the pendant close to the raft. Could Jack and Charlie have crossed the lake?

I stomp up the steep path to the very top. As I reach the peak I glance at the view. I can see the other side of the island which is rocky with lots of small coves. The path leads towards the old sugar mill which I spotted from the boat. I know about sugar plantations in the Caribbean from a geography lesson at school. Mr Rushton showed us a film about how sugar is produced from cane. I never thought I'd see a real sugar mill, ever.

This old sugar mill looks weird. I can see a purple glow coming from a window. I think someone may be in there. I practically run from the top of the hill and down the other side. Amy follows me in hot pursuit. Maybe Charley and Jack are in there. I grab Amy's hand before she can protest and run up the path leading to the ruined building.

As we get closer I can hear voices coming from the glassless window frames. We crouch down behind a pile of old stone and listen.

"Have the next batch arrived yet?" I hear a muffled voice ask.

"Not yet, the storm is slowing things down," a different voice says. "We'll have to wait until the boat can dock."

I wonder what's going on. Who are these people and what are they up to? I need to take a peek. Very slowly I climb onto a rock and lift my head above the window ledge. A beefy man has his back to me and is talking to a woman in a long dress and a big floppy hat. She looks elegant but is smoking a long pipe. I can't see her face fully as it is hidden under the hat. There are four cool girls swishing around in tiny skirts and high heeled shoes. I think these must be the Ru-B-Loo assistants Papa Zakarus was telling us about.

Ru-B-Loos

Then I hear the beefy man say, "Have you dealt with the snooping trespassers?" Oh no! This could be Jack and Charley!

"Yes," says the woman in the hat, as a puff of smoke whooshes out of her pipe. "I have sorted them in the usual way. They won't trouble

70

you now."

"Snooping kids!" the beefy man points to a shelf high on the wall. "Now let's develop the new batch. Pass me the corundum solution, Ru-B-Ella."

Corundum! What's that? I must google it later. Just then my foot slips off the rock and I tumble back into a load of prickly grass.

"More snooping kids!" I hear the man shout. "Get rid of them, NOW!"

EEEK!

I pick myself up out of the scratchy grass. I hear the woman's footsteps stomping towards the door. I shouldn't have put my best friend through all this but I have to find Jack and Charley.

Trapped!

I grab Amy's arm and we run as fast as we can.

We run around the side of the sugar mill and down some slippery steps. I spot a green door which I kick open and drag Amy with me into a musty storage cellar. I can hear footsteps stomping past the door outside. Phew! That was close. I wait a while before it's safe to peep outside. Oh no! The door is stuck. I think we've been locked in. Four grey stone walls surround us.

"Do you think we are going to be turned into Picos now?" I think Amy is convinced the woman who has locked us in here is the voodoo witch, Het Scarrow. I'm still struggling to believe this though. But some people may believe in voodoo magic and I always respect the beliefs of other people. I need a scientific explanation about how things happen. There has got to be an earthly explanation for everything. The job of a good detective is to find out what this is. And I will find out . . . when I get out of this dark, dank dungeon and find my little brother and Charley.

Amy is crouched and shivering in the corner. Bending next to her I rub her trembling shoulders. I'm feeling a bit responsible now for getting us into this mess. Now I've got to get us out. The phone is not an option . . . it's ruined. I think about my video game *Escape Week*. I never thought I'd be doing it for real. I really do need an escape plan now. That'll teach me for being addicted to the game. This is how you play it:

Level A is for Across. The player has to get across a field or lake to reach the next level. Well, we've done that for real.

Level B is for Below and Bend. The player has to duck below an object to find her way out of a situation.

Level C is for Crawl and Climb. The player has to crawl along a dark tunnel or up a slippery chimney.

Level D is for Dip and Dive. The player has to dip into the water and dive down deep to find an object or treasure.

Level E is for Escape. The player has to escape from Zombie Island and avoid capture by Zombie Ogres. The object of the game is to escape before the week is up. A WEEK! I hope I can work out how to get us out of here in less than a week. I can hear my tummy rumbling!

I look around the dungeon. The huge green door is not an option. It's totally stuck or locked from outside.

I look around the huge storage room. Sacks are stacked along one wall. I get up to investigate. Untying the string around the neck of a sack I discover it is filled with dried rice. Now what did Tristan say he did with his phone when he accidentally dropped it down the toilet? I know. He said he put it in a bag of rice to soak up all the moisture and that fixed it. It's worth a try while I'm trying to figure out our next move. I plop my new phone in the sack of rice. As I walk around the room I look for clues, carefully scanning the four grey walls. How can we get out of this grimy place?

"Help me move some of these sacks of rice Amy," I whisper. "There could be something hidden behind them. I grab hold of a heavy sack of rice and drag it away from the wall. By moving the rice sacks we discover an old fireplace. I stick my head inside the blackened hole where the fire once blazed and peep up. YES! There's an old fashioned chimney. We can climb up there. I'll check it out.

"I'm going to climb up here first," I say.

"Why, Lottie?" asks Amy.

"It's my demon plan, Amy," I reply looking into her worried eyes.

"If I think it's safe enough, and if there's an escape route at the top, I'll shout and you can follow." I don't wait for Amy's reply. I only hope the chimney is wide enough and I don't get stuck.

This chimney must have been designed for children to climb. I think they used to send children up chimneys in the olden days. There are child-sized foot holes placed at every stride. I have a long way to climb before I reach the beam of light at the top though and my legs are beginning to ache like mad. I must be about half way by now. Ah! Here is a resting place. I'll just plonk down for a while.

Oh no! I can hear voices. I think the chimney-stack links to another fireplace in the room above the basement room. I sit as still as a statue on a small ledge, crouch inside the fireplace and listen.

"Get your skinny legs over here!" I know that voice. My tummy does a little flip. Oh no, all that effort and I'm now in the same room as the wicked voodoo witch and the Ru-B-Loos and the beefy man.

Sizzling Turtles!

It's then I see it happen. I can see the beefy man. He is working at a bench wearing a white mask over his mouth and a cap on his head like a surgeon about to operate. I can't see his face very well but I'm sure I've seen him somewhere before. On the bench in front of him is a baby turtle. It's stretching out its neck as he is scraping its shell with what looks like a nail file.

He then takes a small knife and dips it in a glass of dusty stuff in front of him. The man smears the dusty stuff from the knife onto the shell of the wiggling baby turtle. He then does something really horrible. He gets a blow-torch. I know it's called a blow-torch because I've seen a chef use one on *Saturday Morning Kitchen*. The chef melted brown sugar on top of a creamy pudding.

The beefy man then flicks on the blow-torch and a bright orange-yellow flame shoots out. My heart almost leaps out of my chest as he blasts the flame over the turtle's shell.

The voodoo witch then stands over the baby turtle. She has a long stick in her hand. She circles the stick over the turtle's shell and begins to chant.

**By the power of Korecky Stone
Tail of rat and lizard bone
Corundum from the underground
Mix together, stick and bound**

75

Red hot fire. . . loggerhead turtle
Heat to make your shell glow purple
A trillion years turn into one
Gem formation has begun
Shining rubies glisten and shine
Red as hearts my Valentine
Glimmering sapphires will grow too
Precious gems of turquoise blue.

Het Scarrow then takes the baby turtle and plops it in a tank with lots of other baby turtles. He hits the water with a crackle, sputter and sizzle! I watch him swim to his friends. He seems okay but I'm sure that must have hurt the little fellow. What are these nasty people doing?

"Okay, Het!" I really do recognise that Scottish voice. The beefy man takes off his mask and turns to face witchy woman. Het! It must be true then. Het Scarrow really does exist. It's then I see beefy man's face. It's Hamish MacDougal . . . that creepy hotel owner. But what is he up to? He speaks to Het Scarrow "We've finished here for today. Have you dealt with those snooping kids yet?" She shakes her head and turns to the Ru-B-Loo girls.

"Ru-B-Loos! Get your skinny legs down to the basement and bring up the latest lot of snooping kids." EEEK! Het Scarrow must have locked the green door after all. The Ru-B-Loos are going to discover Amy down there. I have no choice. I can't carry on climbing to the very top of the chimney to see if there's an escape route. I have to go back down . . . QUICKLY!

The Ru-B-Loos are Tricked

My flip-flopped-feet slip and slide as I scuttle down the chimney. Who will get there first? Phew! My toes land just as the green door creaks open. Four Ru-B-Loos sashay into the basement room like a band of Barbie dolls on a mission. The first one through the door carries a tray of drinks. Four glasses of orange juice are on the tray. Now that's weird because there are only two of us. One of the Ru-B-Loos offers us a drink. Both Amy and I take one. I glance at Amy and shake my head. I'm not sure if we should drink this even though I'm dead thirsty. The same Ru-B-Loo then swishes around and struts out of the door with the other two drinks. Who are they for?

My brain bubbles and fizzes and I remember the words of Papa Zakarus. I reach behind me and grab a handful of the rice from one of the sacks. With one gigantic throw the rice scatters all over the floor. Immediately the Ru-B-Loos dive to the ground to pick up the grains of rice one by one. Magic! Papa Zakarus said that the Ru-B-Loos can do nothing else until every last grain is collected. There are a zillion grains scattered in every dark corner of the cellar. Amy seems to get what I'm doing and copies my action. But the problem is one of the Ru-B-Loos has already left with the tray of drinks. I'll get her later.

Then something funny happens. The grains of rice in the other sack begin to wiggle like squirming maggots! I realise it's my phone vibrating. Tristan's rice trick must have worked. My phone must not have been quite as damaged as his. I'm sure he said it took two days

77

to dry out. This is a bonus. I glance at the screen. It says 'one new message' although I don't know when it was sent. I flick on the text message. It's from Mum.

Where the blinking heck are you?

We are worried to death.

Is Jack with you?

Phone immediately!

Oh no! Mum is upset. That's the thing about Mum; she flips into creative language mode when she's upset. I should have involved the parents from the start. Now I'm in deep trouble. I try to ring her but the signal is dipping in and out. I tap in a message with my speedy thumb.

Hi Mum!

 We R in a bit of trouble.

At the Old Sugar Mill on Turtle Island.

Something funny is going on. Luv L xx

I hit send. One of those annoying symbols pop up displaying *'try again'*. No time to mess with it now. I grab some more rice and stick it in my pocket just in case. We leave the three Ru-B-Loos picking up rice and head out of the door.

I remember the Sacred Pendant and take it out of my pocket. The feathers are twitching like mad. I can see the other Ru-B-Loo girl turning the corner towards a path in the forest. Perhaps Aztilum the wolf spirit is sniffing out Charley's scent from the beanie hat and maybe the Ru-B-Loo girl is taking those drinks to Jack and Charley. There's only one way to find out.

"Quick Amy," I say. We follow the girl in the direction of the twitching feathers.

We are close behind her now and she hasn't spotted us. Time for action! I see a set of keys jingling and jangling on a belt around her waist. I grab as much rice as I can out of my pocket and throw it up in the air above her head. As the rice rains down to the ground she immediately falls to pick up the grains. She is helpless. I grab the keys.

She can't stop me as she has to pick up every last grain of rice. I glance at the twitching feathers on the Sacred Pendant again. They point up a hillside so we climb the hill to the top. Ahead of us is the Plantation House. I saw this on the map when I searched Turtle Island on the internet. The feathers are doing their frantic twitching routine again.

"Come on, Amy. I think that's where Jack and Charley must be." I run ahead. This must be the secret place where children are hidden before they are turned into Picos. We must be quick. We reach the grand house. I glance at the huge front door. This must have been a gorgeous house a hundred years ago. Now the carved woodwork is flaky-grey. I drag Amy by the arm and run around to the rear of the house. We don't want to be seen by anyone. It's so spooky! Suddenly, I hear a small voice say my name.

"Lottie! Over here!" The voice is coming from a metal grate low down beneath a window pane. Crouching down and peeking through the grate I feel a ginormous rush of relief as I see the grubby faces of two normal little boys beaming up at me. Jack and Charley!

Inside the Old Plantation House

I take a monster kick at the metal grate. On the forth kick there's a loud C-R-A-C-K . . . the rusty fittings break away from the opening in the wall. "C'mon Amy, let's climb through," I say.

"But what if we get stuck?" Amy groans. "What if we can't get out of the basement?"

"We'll face that if and when it happens." I get on my knees and begin to duck below the hole in the wall where the grate had been. It's a bit of a squeeze. Jack makes a sobbing sound as he sees my body poke through the hole. He bends down to hug me before I can drag my legs through. I think he's pleased to see me for once. I stand up and hug him to my chest. Thank goodness he is still a real boy. His nose is still in the middle of his face and his bottom is just where a bottom should be. Just then Amy pokes her body through the hole in the wall. Charley Marley bends down to give her the Wadadidili greeting. I give Charley his beanie hat and he plonks it on his head.

After all the hugging and high-five-knuckle-rubbing routine we plonk on the floor. I need to think of our next move. I text Mum again and I hope there's some phone signal.

Jack and Charley are safe!

That's all I have time for. I hit send. Fingers crossed.

"C'mon! We have to get out of here."

80

* * *

I remember the keys in my pocket and try the basement door. Luckily, it opens! A flight of stairs leads to a corridor. I hear strange whispers echo through the empty corridor. Sneaking along, we creep past rows of arched doorways. The whispers are becoming louder in my ears. Following the muffled sounds we reach a flaky-painted door. I inch the door open just a little bit more and peep into the room. The elegant lady in the straw hat and four different Ru-B-Loos are standing with their backs to me. I can't see what they are doing but I hear crunching sounds.

Then I see something horrible.

I back away quietly on my tip-toes making frantic hand signals to the others to leave quickly.

Voodoo Hit!

I feel a rush of relief to see Papa Zakarus waiting by the edge of Wobblite Lake.

"Well done my friends," Papa Zakarus says. He points to a bush for us to take cover. "Come, let's hide." Running like mad to escape from the Plantation House has almost popped my lungs. I can hear the beating of my heart in my ears. Did she see us? Are they following us?

Safely crouching behind the tamarind tree, Papa Zakarus seems to think we are safe . . . for now. Turning to Jack and Charley he says, "I don't think we've met." He holds out a claw to Charley.

"It's okay," I say to Charley, as I see the scared expression on his face. I'm still panting.

Trying to present a tough guy image he gives Papa Zakarus the official Wadadidili greeting, clasping his claw and then shaking and banging knuckles together. "Hi! I'm Charley Marley."

"Charley Marley, I know your grandmother well," says Papa Zakarus. "She was a good friend of mine. I used to live on the island of Wadadidili many years ago. I know she is a good person."

"She will kill me once she knows I am here," says Charley.

"I think not," says Papa Zakarus. "Once she knows you are safely with me she will be pleased."

I peek through the branches and flame-red flowers of the bush. It's then I see the elegant lady whose poised figure and dress make her appear beautiful. She must have spotted us snooping around the Plantation House and discovered her prisoners have escaped. I still can't see her face clearly because she is wearing the large straw hat which keeps it in dim shadow. She is muttering some strange sounding words in-between puffing on an enormous pipe. Great plumes of smoke waft all around her.

"Amphibiante dela poisonetto . . . pico nimo antirubianos . . ." She seems to be chanting some kind of foreign language as she approaches the tree we are huddled behind.

We are perfectly still and quiet, not daring to waft an eyelash.

Het Scarrow is Coming!

"That, my friends is Het Scarrow," Papa Zakarus whispers.

"But she doesn't look that scary, she looks beautiful," whispers Amy.

"My dear friend, Amy, you have not seen what is under that hat. She is an evil person . . . very evil," whispers Papa Zakarus glancing at his claws. Het Scarrow is now so close to us I catch a whiff of her niffy-smoky breath. Eeek!

It's then the attack begins.

Papa Zakarus bounds out of the bush. Het Scarrow stops in front of Papa Zakarus. Izzy-Lizzy crawls onto her foot.

"Get away . . . you horrible creature or I'll have you in the pot for dinner," she shouts at the iguana. Izzy-Lizzy replies by biting her big toe.

"Ouch! You green, scaly monster," screams Het. I swallow a giggle and daren't even look at Amy as we keep statue-still.

"Good afternoon, Het," Papa Zakarus says, "It's been a long time since we spoke together. How are you?"

"I'd be a lot better if I didn't have a sore toe, Zakarus," she replies, "What brings you to my side of the island?" She called him Zakarus because that was the name she knew him by before she left Wadadidili.

"I wasn't aware that any part of the island could be owned by you or anyone else, my dear," says Papa Zakarus calmly. As he speaks Het tries to hide her face even more under the hat.

"Well, I would prefer it if you left me alone now, I have work to do," she says turning her back on him. Choppa's wings flutter so fast they look like little rainbows in the air. Papa Zakarus waves his clawed hand at the hummingbird. Choppa sweeps down and whisks the straw hat from Het Scarrow's head taking three strands of hair with it.

There is a long silence followed by a loud gasp! Whoa! Het Scarrow is so ugly. Her hideous face is covered in oozing boils. Her pointed ears drip with dark brown wax and her eyes . . . her eyes are the worst . . . they seem invisible! There are two black beans where her eyeballs should be. She's as bald as a boiled egg apart from four hairs spiking on top. How hideous, revolting and repulsive! Ugh!

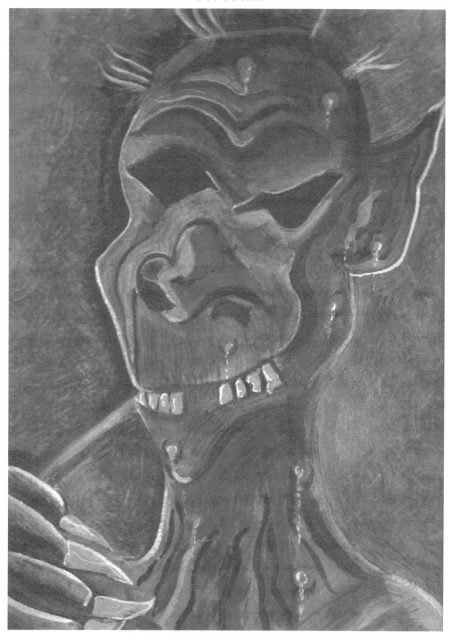

Ugh! Ugly Het Scarrow!

"Go on! Take a good look at me!" She shouts with rage at Papa Zakarus.

"You're no oil painting yourself!"

"You have a chance to make things better Het," Papa Zakarus says, "I know what you and Hamish MacDougal are doing to the island and its inhabitants. Undo the spell that keeps the children imprisoned as Picos and promise not to take any more children captive. You are destroying the beautiful environment of this paradise with your greed and ambition. What happiness is it bringing you anyway?"

"It gives me beauty in a way I don't have any more," she wails. "I once had everything!" She lunges forward as if to grab him but Papa Zakarus is too quick for her and steps to one side. Het screams at him, "Go! Go leave me in peace before I cast another spell on you."

"You couldn't get it right the first time, woman," says Papa Zakarus. He picks up her straw hat and hands it to her. She rams it onto her head, blows a plume of smoke into his face and turns on her heels to stomp back towards the Plantation House.

"Phew! Do you think she saw us, Papa Zakarus?" I creep out from my hiding place.

"She probably senses you were here. You need to go back to Wadadidili quickly," he says.

"Did she really put a spell on you?" Jack asks.

"Let me tell you about it before you go and then you will understand how dangerous she is. You will keep away from Turtle Island for good. Get the sack of wobbits from behind the tree. We will take the old wooden raft across Wobblite Lake." Everybody steps onto the wobbly raft and sits down. Charley grabs the oar to row us across the lake. Papa Zakarus tells us another of his stories.

Papa Zakarus: His Second Story

"When I was seventeen I fell in love with Het. We lived on the island of Wadadidili. She was my best girl. She was beautiful then and I loved her very much. We used to dance together on the beach at night to the music that came from the hotel. Then one day a rich British scientist named Hamish MacDougal came to stay at the hotel. He owned a large motor boat and would take her on trips. They came over to Turtle Island. I never did trust him. One day she asked me if I wanted to go to Turtle Island with them.

"Still, I began to enjoy the trips too. One day, Hamish MacDougal disappeared for the day and left us alone. Het and I had a great day together. We swam in Wobblite Lake. That's when I found out about Het's allergy to wobbits, the jelly-fish eggs. She came out in a red itchy rash all over and started to be sick.

"For the next few months, on every Saturday, Hamish MacDougal would take us on the boat to Turtle Island. He would go off somewhere and we would swim in the sea and have a picnic on the beach. Then one particular Saturday something weird happened. I would never return to Wadadidili again. We had finished our picnic. Het stood up and said she had to go somewhere and would I mind staying on the beach to wait for her. I waited for a while but soon became bored and thirsty so I began to search for a coconut so I could drink its sweet milk.

"I spotted Het going into the Old Plantation House. I was curious so I followed her. That's when I saw something that shocked and frightened me. I was shaking with anger. Suddenly, I felt a sharp pain on my head. I remember waking up on the beach where Het had left me. I looked down at my hands. They were the hands of a wild animal. My foot was the hoof of a beast and my whole body was covered in fur. I felt at my throbbing head. It had horns protruding from it.

"I later discovered Hamish MacDougal was doing nasty experiments on the island. Het had fallen in love with him and would do anything he asked. I didn't know she had been dabbling in voodoo for some time. I worked out that she had cast a wicked voodoo spell on me."

"But why would she do that?" I ask. I wonder if the horrible thing Papa Zakarus saw at the Plantation House was the same horrible thing I had seen earlier.

"Het wanted to make sure that I didn't go back to Wadadidili to tell anyone about what I had seen. She had intended to turn me into a beast but she was not fully proficient in magic. She got part of the spell wrong. That, my friends, is why I am half man and half beast now."

"So did Het go back to Wadadidili or just stay here on Turtle Island?" Amy asks.

"She went back a few times but then another of her voodoo spells went wrong. She tried to give herself everlasting beauty and eternal youth. The spell required the tails of six iguanas and the wings of three hummingbirds. At the last moment a hummingbird and an iguana escaped and the voodoo spell went wrong," Papa Zakarus goes on. "Het hadn't realized there were not enough ingredients to do the final part of the spell and instead of becoming eternally beautiful she became horrendously ugly."

"Let me guess, Choppa and Izzy-Lizzy are the hummingbird and iguana that escaped," I say bouncing from foot to foot.

"Yes, you've guessed it. Just before they escaped, they were touched by all the ingredients of Het's spell, and so the voodoo worked properly on them rather than on her. It turns out they are the ones that have gained eternal youth," Papa Zakarus explains as we reach the other side of the lake. "They both help me now and warn me if Het Scarrow is around. We try to prevent her from hurting anyone else. We need to stop Hamish MacDougal from doing what he is doing. I also need your assistance to try and reverse the voodoo spell she has cast on the Picos."

Everybody jumps off the raft and Papa Zakarus walks towards a palm tree. "I need your help with this." He plucks a palm leaf from the tree and prepares a message by etching into its surface with his knife. He then tugs two strands of hair from his claws and wraps the leaf around them. "I want you to give this to your grandmother Charley." Charley puts the leaf safely under his beanie hat.

"Now you must go my friends. I will accompany you to the beach." Papa Zakarus begins to walk up the steep hill. I remember the sack of Wobbits and carry them up the hill, then tuck them behind a tree. We all trudge down the hill to Sandy Bay. I'm relieved to see the jet-ski is still where I parked it.

"Charley, can you drive a jet-ski?" I ask.

"Of course I can. I'm the best jet-skier on Wadadidili. The attendants let me drive them all the time when the guests have gone for dinner." He beams his best grin at me.

"Great! Take the jet-ski with Jack and get help while we wait here." I need to get my little brother to safety then I'll deal with the rest of it. "Jack, will you please tell Mum and Dad we are safe?" I say. One teeny-weeny lie will calm the parents down. "And will you ask Tristan and Katie-Louise to come alone in the dive boat and to load on the dive kits. Don't tell anyone else okay?"

"Not even Mum or Dad?" asks Jack.

"It's a secret and I'll tell you later if my plan works out. Go! The sea is calm now and it's still light!" Charley jumps on the front of the jet-ski.

"This is wicked!" says Charley. Jack jumps on the back and clings to Charley's waist. Charley revs up the control throttle and whoosh, off they go.

"I think you are safe now girls. Stay here and wait. I'd better get the raft back to the other side before Het realizes it's missing. "Goodbye and take good care."

Goodbye, Papa Zakarus and thank you for everything. Take care Choppa and Izzy-Lizzy." I watch as his huge shape disappears up the path that leads back through the forest. He thinks we will wait for help. There's no way I'm getting off Turtle Island until I've solved this mystery. And that's that!

The Magic Spell

Granny Marley

Granny Marley looks up from her rocking chair on the balcony of her house. She isn't surprised at all to see the duppy bird waddling towards her. Evil is in the air. Looking out to sea she spots the jet-ski whooshing towards the shore.

"Charley!" she yells.

"Granny Marley!" Charley and Jack leap off the jet-ski and rush towards her. Charley gives her a massive hug. He hands her the leaf as Papa Zakarus told him. She opens it up and reads the carved letters:

M o D

OBEAH

P.Z.

"Charley, Jack hurry now! Get help for Lottie and Amy." Granny Marley knows what she has to do.

* * *

Lottie and Amy

"I hope help arrives soon. It's going to be dark when the sun sets." Amy says in her wimpiest voice ever. I don't blame her. I give a little shiver. There's still no signal on the phone. I wish we could get 3G as I really need to search something.

"Don't worry, Amy. I have a plan."

"You always have a plan, Lottie, but this one isn't working out too well is it?"

I ignore her.

"Come on, Amy. We need to get to the top of that hill again so I can get some signal. If I can get a text through to Tristan or Katie-Louise they can google something for me before they leave the hotel."

"But Papa Zakarus said we had to stay here and wait for help to arrive."

"Well, Papa Zakarus isn't a detective is he? Come on, we have to be brave." I climb back up the hill and follow the forest path again. Het Scarrow has probably gone to bed now anyway. She's *like* one hundred years old. As I reach the top of the hill looking down on Wobblite Lake I sit on a rock and tap in a message to Tristan.

Hi can u google something 4 me?

I tap the keys on my phone, write what it is I want him to search and hit send. I stand on the rock and wave my phone about in the air. Good! There's one bar flickering. The message is delivered by cyber magic!

The view is stunning from here. I hear an engine sound. I hope Jack and Charley have returned safely and found Tristan and Katie-Louise by now. Perhaps it's them already. I can see a boat approaching the bay close to the Plantation House but it doesn't look like the dive boat. But it is a boat I've seen before.

"Look!" Amy yells. At first I thought she had spotted the boat too. But oh no! She's spotted something scarier. Het Scarrow! She's heading our way.

I feel tiny pin-pricks of horror as she stands up close. She holds my eyes in a scary gaze with her black-beanie eyes. I stare at the cluster of oozing yellow boils on her face and the three brown teeth protruding from each side of her salivating mouth. Ugh! I feel sick.

"Now you can't escape me you horrible children," Het Scarrow growls. Het then raises a long fingernail and points at me and Amy in turn. "I will turn you into my children . . . my Picos, so you can work on this island forever. Yesss," the words hiss through the old hag's pinched lips like a snake. Her eyes suddenly flash vivid purple. **Yikes!** She takes a huge puff of her long pipe then makes an ear-piercing witchy laugh. We're doomed!

* * *

Granny Marley

Granny Marley takes the leaf-parcel inside her house built on stilts. She reads the strange letters again and knows exactly what to do. The sun is about to set. She needs to work quickly or it will be too late.

From under her bed she reaches for an old box. Opening it she takes out the old rag doll she had owned since she was a child. Next to it is a strange looking stick. She hadn't touched this in a long time.

Many years earlier, the two friends had spent time each making a doll. She had made her doll look like her best friend and had even used a piece of Hetty's old dress to make a skirt for it. Granny Marley now takes the doll and plaits the strands of hair, that were wrapped in the leaf-parcel Charley had brought to her, into the wool hair on the rag doll.

Granny Marley looks again at the message.

M. o. D

OBEAH

PZ

PZ! This is from her old friend Zakarus who disappeared from Wadadidili years ago. Zakarus was nicknamed *Papa Zakarus* by all his friends because he always took care of the animals on the island. She works out that 'M.O.D.' means *Mother of Darkness* and knows exactly who that is. Hetty, her best friend. She had become a maker of dark voodoo magic. The next part of the message spells out *'OBEAH'*. From her own knowledge of voodoo she realizes this means an obeah stick. Years ago, Granny Marley had been given Eliza Kinty's own obeah stick. An obeah stick is the voodoo version of a magic wand. Voodoo vibes tingle through her finger tips as her hand slides along the smooth mahogany wood. Carved into the shaft is a special crest; a crow is carrying a snake in its claws. On the very end there is the foot of a chicken.

Eliza Kinty chose well. Granny Marley had learnt everything about the good voodoo and is now the new Mother of Brightness.

Granny Marley

It is time to dress in the Mother of Brightness robes. The ancient voodoo necklace is made from banana palms and parrot beaks. She carefully hangs it around her neck. Voodoo magic is a tricky thing. It's easy to get spells wrong with terrible results. The tip of the sun is about to disappear beyond the horizon. Timing is everything.

Waving the obeah stick over the rag doll she chants the spell:

'The Destruction of Evil Beings.'

"Mother of Darkness and evil curses
Take heed of these more powerful verses
Halt your evil this moment in time
Be gone forever your power of swine
Chattering Blue birds and Giant Bamboo
May we see the very end of YOU?"

With that she made three more circles with the obeah stick and plunged it into the rag doll. The sun dipped over the sea. The spell had been cast.

* * *

Lottie and Amy

I remember the sack of jelly-fish eggs. It's our one and only chance of stopping this mad witch. "Quick Amy, grab the sack of wobbits." I point to the tree where the sack had been hidden. We both reach into the sack and grab a handful of the jelly-fish eggs. I chuck a gooey handful into the witch's ugly mug. What a shot! Wham! The slimy jelly goo smashes into her eyes and plops down her face.

Amy lobs a handful of wobbits and one goes straight into Het

Scarrow's pipe. Her ugly face turns purple as she sucks in the smoke. The horrible boils ooze more yellow stinking pus. Het Scarrow twitches and scratches, leaping about from foot to foot.

"You horrible child-gang!" she growls. Then it happens . . .

Lime green lights zip and whiz above her head!

Then . . . Whooooosh!

Het Scarrow disappears before our eyes leaving a gooey green puddle on the ground.

Wow!

Great shot Amy!

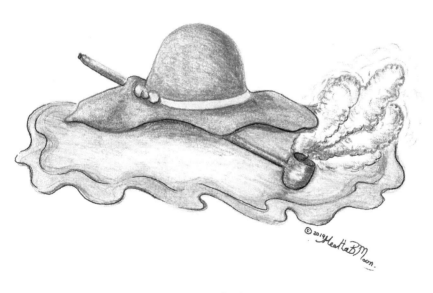

Vanished!

Back to Wobblite Lake

I am alive. This is actually quite surprising. I've known people to be allergic to things. I suffer awful hay fever during the summer but I never knew an allergy to be *that* serious. This place is so weird. Now Het Scarrow has been exterminated I need to work quickly.

A good detective needs to tie up the loose ends. I make a mental list of what I need to do.

1. I need to find this big diamond thingie. The Korecky-Nimo Diamond is essential for reversing Het Scarrow's wicked spells.

2. Picos need to become normal children again.

3. Poor Papa Zakarus needs to become a full man again.

4. And . . . I need to save the turtles.

I haven't told Amy what I saw in that room yet. It will upset her and she's already a nervous wreck on this island. But it is horrible. I have some ideas buzzing around my head but I need to be absolutely certain before I involve anyone else. I hope Tristan managed to get the information I need from the internet. Talking of Tristan, I can hear a boat's engine noise.

"Come on, Amy! They're here." We dash back down the hill to Sandy Bay just as the boat is docking. I run into the sea before they can even get ashore. Better not wet my phone again!

"What on earth happened here?" says Tristan. He looks at me with the widest grin on his face. I can't imagine what I look like. My red curls are such a tangled mess I'll never get a comb through my hair ever.

98

"If I even begin to tell you, you'll think I'm mad."

"You're mad anyway girl," he grins.

"I'll explain as we go but first did you find out about it?"

"Yes, it was a strange request though, but I'll show you." Tristan flicks his phone on and shows me the information I need.

"Great! Thanks Tristan," I'll explain everything as we go. "Have you brought the dive gear?"

"Yes, it's all in the boat."

"Good, we need to lug it up the hill. We have a night-dive to do in a freshwater jelly-fish lake." I say. Amy's face has turned the colour of pale custard again. We each grab some of the heavy dive-gear and climb up and over the hill to the lake.

Luckily the raft is still where Het Scarrow left it on this side of Wobblite Lake. We load on the dive gear. The silver feathers are doing the twitching-fluttering-mad routine. I think I know why they flutter.

I hope I'm right.

Horrible Discovery!

Drifting across the lake on the raft I have time to look at the information on Tristan's phone. The answer to my question is right here. Tristan had googled: *'**What is Corundum?**'*

Corundum is a crystalline form of aluminium oxide typically containing traces of iron, titanium, vanadium and chromium. It is a rock-forming mineral.

My suspicions are confirmed. I know what that nasty Hamish MacDougal is doing to the turtles. With the help of Het Scarrow's evil magic he is growing precious jewels on the shells of turtles. As the raft reaches the other side of the lake I say, "I have discovered something horrible."

"Is it something you saw in that room, Lottie?" Amy asks.

"Yes, Amy. Let's unload the dive gear and leave it here. We'll walk up to the Old Plantation House and I'll show you." The light is dwindling so we grab the diving torches from the equipment bags and tiptoe around the back of the house. Everything is the same. No one has fixed the metal grate. Flashing my torch-light through the grate I see the door to the stairs is still open. I hope the whispering sounds have gone too. "Through here!" I point to the grate.

"Here we go again," Amy whispers under her breath. We climb through the gap one by one and tiptoe up the stairs by torchlight. I can't hear the whispering sounds but I do hear a grunting sound echoing down the long corridor.

"Now which of these arched doors leads to that horrid room?" I swish around to the others who are following me closely.

"I'm not sure Lottie," Amy whispers, "so we'll peep in each one as we go." This is a good idea.

The first door we peep through is filled with small camp beds. Gentle snoring sounds are coming from the Ru-B-Loos. I carefully close the door.

The second door we peep through has an empty bed against the far wall. Weird dream-catchers made of dead chicken feet, parrot beaks and bird feathers hang from the ceiling. This must be Het Scarrow's room. She won't need it now!

The grunting sound is getting louder. Grunt . . . Wheeeeeze . . . GRUNT . . . Wheeeeeze! I gingerly open the third door. A gigantic four-poster bed rules the center of the room. It's the kind of bed from fairytales like the giant's bed in Jack and the Beanstalk. It even comes complete with beefy giant under the quivering duvet. He sounds like a grunting gorilla. Then I realise it's the great lunk, Hamish MacDougal! I put a wobbly finger to my lips, make a hushing sound and gently close the door. Please, please stay asleep, you big oaf!

We sneak along the corridor and I slowly open the next door. It creaks like a squeaky mouse. Shining my torch into the corner of the room I see them. "This is the room!" A chunk of ice plops nastily in my tummy.

"Ugh!" Katie-Louise gulps.

"Oh no!" Tristan gasps.

"I feel sick!" Amy sobs.

The shells of dead turtles are still piled high in the corner of the room.

"What's going on here?" Katie-Louise creeps towards the shells. Her fingers tremble as she holds her torch close and slides her quivering hands over one of them. "The shells have been hacked," she cries. I run my hand along a shell and poke a finger into a jagged hole. It's horrific! My eyes begin to prick.

"I've worked out what is happening here but there's no time to explain now." I glance at Katie-Louise, Amy and Tristan in turn. Tears glisten on their cheeks too. "We really have to do a night-dive in the lake. Are you all up for it?"

We head back to the edge of Wobblite Lake and I explain what we are looking for.

"Can I stay and keep watch?" Amy asks.

"That's a good idea, Amy." I say. I know she's nervous at the best of times so I'm not going to put my best friend through any more scary situations than are absolutely necessary. "You keep watch and shine your torch down through the lake's surface in an emergency." Everyone else kits up. At this point of the dive we usually have Marcus the dive instructor giving us the brief but Tristan and Katie-Louise are qualified P.A.D.I. divers so if the three of us stick together everything will be okay. I show them the Sacred Pendant. It's time to explain what's going on.

"This is the Sacred Pendant. You have to trust me as we have no time to explain the full story." I say. "I'll hold it and Katie-Louise will you shine the torch-light on the feathers. We must follow the direction of where the feathers are pointing."

"What are we looking for?" Tristan asks.

"We are searching for the Korecky-Nimo Diamond. Het Scarrow hid it somewhere and I think it could be in Wobblite Lake. Every time the Sacred Pendant is over the lake the feathers do their nutty twitching routine. The Korecky-Nimo Diamond fits here." I point to the gap where the missing gem should be. "When the Sacred Pendant is complete it is the most powerful thing in the islands and will break the evil spells cast by Het Scarrow." Tristan is doing his best eye roll.

"Just do it Tristan!" yells Katie-Louise. "It all sounds like mumbo-jumbo now but I'm sure Lottie will tell us more when we have time." I like Katie-Louise. She doesn't stand for any rubbish. We hand Amy our phones and wade into the inky water of Wobblite Lake.

Twinkling Turtles

The water is absolutely freeze-bobs! It's pitch-black. Things are different at night than scuba diving in the crystal clear Caribbean Sea during the daytime. It's hairy-scary! I'm not sure which way I am facing at first . . . up or down? My eyes begin to adjust to the darkness as I stare through my mask. Oh my goodness! Jelly-fish surround me! I have to be brave. What's a little sting or two compared to the suffering of those turtles?

When I realized what Hamish MacDougal was doing I worked it all out. I saw the turtle on our last dive. He gobbled up the jelly-fish for his dinner. The turtles must be here, there's food for them. It's where nasty Hamish MacDougal is keeping them in captivity and feeding them to grow to full size. I'd spotted a flash of something when we swam across the lake with Papa Zakarus.

Just then my torch light catches a flash of blue and red. Rainbow lights flash around me. I focus my eyes and shine my torch. The lake is full of them. Turtles everywhere! Twinkling turtles! Glittering turtle shells encrusted with dazzling gems. I am right!

I shine my torch back to the Sacred Pendant. The feathers are pointing in all directions. It seems confused. Up and down they go one minute, then side to side the next.

Suddenly I stop swimming. All the silver feathers are pointing in the direction of one turtle in particular. I swim alongside the huge turtle. In the center of its shell, is the largest, most sparkling, glittering diamond. It is a zillion times bigger than the one in Mum's engagement ring. So that is where Het Scarrow hid the Korecky-Nimo diamond. Clever! The turtle doesn't swim away from me. I hold onto its fin and reach to the middle of its shell to hold the diamond.

At that precise moment the Sacred Pendant glows purple in the dark depths of the deep water. Aztilum the wolf image opens his mouth wide then snaps it shut. The gigantic diamond is released from the turtle's shell into my hand. As I let go of the turtle's fin he seems to smile as he swims away to join his friends.

Grasping the huge gem in my hand I give the thumb-up signal to surface.

Professor Tartan Underpants!

Amy is sitting by the edge of the lake as we wade out of the water. I hold out the Korecky-Nimo Diamond for them all to see.

"Wow!" Everyone gasps together as the diamond gleams in the palm of my hand.

We take off the heavy tanks and dive kit and I put the gem carefully in my zip-up pocket. Just then a voice booms out. Oh no!

"Hey you! What do you think you're doing?" Hamish MacDougal is huffing and puffing down the hill dressed only in his tartan underpants and a pair of the most ridiculous furry tartan slippers. If he had not been so scary Amy and I would be laughing out loud. He's waving his arms in the air. As he gets closer I can see his beetroot face. He is breathing like a winded hippopotamus.

Professor Tartan Underpants! ... Hamish MacDougal

"You meddling kids! What are you doing with my turtles?"

"Turtles don't belong to anyone!" Our eyes lock. "You are a very greedy man. I know what you're doing." I stand right in front of him and glare into his eyes. Creep!

It's then the weird attack happens. Hamish MacDougal shoots out a snatching hand. He is about to grab me but just then Papa Zakarus bounds out of the dark. He grasps the beefy man's feet and rugby-tackles him to the ground. Izzy-Lizzy scratches at a long tree creeper on the ground. I grab the creeper and wrap it around the hands of the wheezing Scottish scientist while Papa Zakarus holds him down.

"I know just the punishment for you. Nasty beefy man!" I say as Papa Zakarus ties his feet and drags him onto the old raft.

Tristan and Katie-Louise's eyes boggle and stare at the beast-man. What happens next is totally bizarre. I take the Korecky-Nimo Diamond from my pocket and show it to Papa Zakarus. His face crinkles into a wrinkly smile.

"Lottie, place the Korecky-Nino Diamond back in its setting in the Sacred Pendant to give Aztilum the ultimate power," Papa Zakarus says. "Then it will then break the evil voodoo spell to release the Picos and return me to my original form." I take the Sacred Pendant from my neck and pop the diamond in the hole.

POW! FLASH! An exploding bomb!

I can't see a thing through the cloud of purple smoke. Then the night air clears. Out of the dark stands a tall handsome man with black curly hair and smooth dark skin. Papa Zakarus is the beast-man no longer. The horns have gone from his head and the claws have disappeared from his fingertips. The fur has left his body and he has two human legs. A full-man again!

"You look amazing, dude!" gasps Tristan. You could use another trainer shoe though."

"Thank you my friend, maybe I can buy a pair at the market when I go back to Wadadidili. Now I can see all my old friends," says Papa Zakarus in the same gentle voice as before.

At that precise moment I hear the yells and giggles of children. Twenty or more kids are waving at us from the other side of the moonlit lake.

"The Picos!" yells Amy, "Look! They are normal children again."

The bad spell has been broken.

"The Sacred Pendant **is** the most powerful weapon ever against evil voodoo now it includes the Korecky Nimo," I say.

"Yes, it's like your dad says," Amy jokes, "It's all inclusive!"

"Come on, everyone. Let's get this creep to Wadadidili and turn him in to the Caribbean police. I have gathered enough evidence to get him arrested along with his accomplices."

"Who are his accomplices?" asks Amy.

"I will tell you all when I do my summing-up meeting at the Sunset Bar," I say. "A good detective always ties up the loose ends. Now I know what to do with *him* on our way." I turn to Tristan. "It's not possible for us all to sail across the lake on the raft. Could you take Professor Tartan Underpants here and the girls back to Sandy Bay and return for me and Papa Zakarus? I need to collect some evidence."

Vital Evidence!

As the others drift across Wobblite Lake I grab hold of Papa Zakarus by his soft hand. "Will you come with me?"

"Of course, Lottie my friend. I think I know what you need to gather."

We walk back up the hill to the Old Plantation House. This time I know exactly which door it is. Collecting a turtle shell is not a pleasant thing to do but it's necessary. I then peep through the other door where the Ru-B-Loos sleep. Suppressing a giggle I gather more evidence in a pillow case. This is so weird. Wait till I show Amy!

"I've got everything I need but next we have to take the path to Turtle Bay," I say.

"It's quite a dangerous climb down the rocks Lottie." He looks at me with his kind eyes.

"Yes, but it's absolutely necessary Papa Zakarus." We take the path that leads from the back of the Old Plantation House towards Turtle Bay. As we reach the cliff edge I gaze down to the tiny beach. It's as I thought. *Highlander* is tethered to a buoy. I hear the trickle of water from Wobblite Lake as it flows out to sea. So why are the turtles not escaping from the lake?

Just then Izzy-Lizzy scratches at something on the edge of the rock face. It's a rope. Tugging at the rope I drag it up from the cliff edge. Dangling on the end is a large tub filled with empty bags. Chopper the hummingbird swoops down to the beach below. He wants in on the action. Chopper hovers over the beach and scoops something up in his long, pointy beak. He flies back and hovers close to me. As I hold out my hand he drops a little stone into my palm saving me from the dangerous climb. It glitters and gleams in the moonlight. On closer inspection I see it is a ruby-red gem.

"I think I have the final piece of the puzzle now." I turn to Papa Zakarus and beam my best Lottie Lovall International Investigator smile. Loaded up with evidence we go back to the lake and wait for Tristan to take us back to the other side.

Freedom!

Giggling children are doing a happy moonlight dance by the light of the moon. Their eyes, noses, mouths, feet and bottoms are all in the normal places. Soon we can return them all to Wadadidili. Their parents will be happy too. They skip alongside us as we climb the hill back to Sandy Bay. As we arrive there, I notice Hamish MacDougal has already been dumped into the dive boat and tied to a bench.

Papa Zakarus looks at him and beams his huge smile, but now his skin is smooth. He turns back to me. "It's time to tell your friends exactly what that bad man has been doing to the turtles Lottie. I will see you soon," he says. "I'm going to stay here with the children until they are shipped back to their parents. I'll become Keeper of Turtle Island and live in the Old Plantation House. Everything needs some tender loving care."

"I agree," I say. "What do you say Chopper and Izzy-Lizzy?" They reply with a buzz of wings and a scratch of my foot. I give Papa Zakarus a gigantic hug and Amy does the same.

"Thank you for protecting us and helping us to find Jack and Charley, Papa Zakarus," I say.

"You have Aztilum to thank for showing you the way." He beams his dazzling smile again. "Please give the Sacred Pendant to Charley's grandmother. She will keep it safe and put it to good use." Choppa hums ahead and up the hill. Papa Zakarus follows and Izzy-Lizzy scuttles on behind.

* * *

"We'd better get back to Wadadidili now," says Katie-Louise. "Your parents must be frantic, Lottie. The Caribbean police will be sending out a search party."

"Yes, they will," I say. I twist around to face Tristan. "Before we go can you drive the boat around the headland to Turtle Bay? There's something we must do. I'll explain everything but please hurry."

"You snooping, meddling kids!" snaps Hamish MacDougal. I go up to him and glare into his evil eyes.

"You are a nasty man and I'm going to show everyone what you've been doing," I say. I hold the tiny ruby in my fingers. "This look familiar, creep?" I point to the turtle shell. "Exactly how much money did you make out of their suffering?" My heart is pounding in my chest. He turns his head away from me. "Yes, should be ashamed of yourself."

"What exactly has he done, Lottie?" Tristan asks. Time to explain!

"Well, you know when I asked you to google *corundum* for me?" A loud groan comes from Hamish MacDougal.

"Yes, I thought it was a strange request," says Tristan. "It's some kind of mineral isn't it?"

"Yes, Hamish MacDougal has a laboratory at the sugar mill. He was using corundum there. Corundum is a material found in rock formation. Rubies and sapphires are formed out of the mineral corundum. Rubies are red due to the presence of chromium and sapphires are usually blue."

"But what has all this got to do with the turtles?" Amy asks.

"He's been stealing the turtle eggs and hatchlings." There was a loud gasp from everyone. "This creep has been growing precious jewels on the backs of turtles," I say pointing at The Creep.

"But how is that possible?" Tristan asks.

Katie-Louise pipes up, "The turtle's shell is covered in scutes that are made of keratin, the same stuff our fingernails are made of," says

Katie-Louise. "New scutes grow by the addition of keratin layers to the base of each scute."

"Exactly!" I say. Katie-Louise knows a lot about turtles. I know that scutes make up the square patterns on a turtle's shell. "I saw him scrape holes into the shell of the baby turtle. He then implanted specks of corundum into its shell."

"So what was he doing with the blow-torch?" Amy asks.

"As the turtle shell is forming he puts it through the precise conditions that need to exist to create sapphires and rubies." I reply, feeling clever because I'd discovered this when I read the information Tristan had found on the internet. "Over 150 million years ago, rocks inside the earth's surface were subjected to intense pressure and heat to create deposits of sapphire and ruby." I said it just as I remembered the information. I'm beginning to sound like a real detective now. "So, The Creep here used the blow-torch to imitate the process. The turtles are growing at a fast rate and the sapphire and ruby deposits are forming as they grow. That's why he needed turtle shells to produce the jewels, nothing else would do. With the right conditions and by adding more corundum the gems are ready to be harvested in just less than three years."

"Cruel or what?" says Katie-Louise. "So where is he keeping these jewelled turtles?"

"He keeps the babies in tanks inside the sugar mill. Then they are transferred to Wobblite Lake to feed on jelly-fish and grow to full size. The jewels grow in size too." I say. "I suspect the overflow from the lake to the sea has been blocked off so the turtles can't escape. That's why we need to go to Turtle Bay now."

"What are we waiting for? C'mon." Tristan starts up the engine and we whizz around the headland to Turtle Bay. As we reach the small beach I am the first to leap out of the boat. I run straight to the outlet from the lake where the water flows out to the sea. Someone *has* blocked it off with a metal grate. I think I know that person. The Creep!

113

I kick the grate. Tristan kicks the grate. We all kick the grate until . . . CRACK! It eventually gives way. First one turtle pops out into the flowing water . . . then another. Sparkling jewelled shells glisten and gleam in the moonlit night. They remind me of the turtle magnet on our fridge at home. But these are real, living creatures. Whoosh! Off they go, triggering streaky, gleaming rainbows in celebration of their freedom.

I glance into the *Highlander*. The bottom of the boat is littered with fishing nets and empty bags. I'll leave those bits of evidence for The Caribbean Forensics Team.

* * *

Now to punish The Creep, 'Lottie Lovall Style'! On our return to Wadadidili I ask Tristan to drive the boat to the island of plastic rubbish. Plastic Island is still as horrible as before. Tristan slows the engine.

Amy and Katie-Louise grab Hamish MacDougal's feet. Tristan and I grab him under his armpits. He's such a heavy, wiggling blob! We lob Hamish MacDougal into the pile of filthy garbage. Straight under the bobbing rubbish he goes . . . Splash!

"Ha-ha! That's what I call tossing the caber," says Tristan. Hamish MacDougal lifts his ugly head from the trash, spitting and spluttering. He dangles from the boat by the tree creeper rope. Very appropriate for such a creep! Bobbing around his head are the coffee-cup lids, the toy dinosaur, yogurt pots, cheap plastic rain coat and loads of old flip-flops.

"Right!" I say to Tristan, "Steer the boat very slowly through the plastic waste." Tristan does exactly this. Hamish MacDougal is dragged through the disgusting junk. As his head dips up and down revolting things stick to his hair. He's yelling and screaming but just then a dirty baby's nappy whacks him in the mouth. It sticks to his face. He looks like The Poo Monster! "C'mon," I say, "Let's get The Creep back to

Wadadidili for the Caribbean police to deal with."

The Creep!

Presents and Pancakes

The tangerine sun pops up over the horizon as we approach the shoreline of Wadadidili. Mum, Dad, Nana, Pop, Jack and Charley are waving like mad. As we get closer I can see the strained, anxious faces. My parents! I jump out of the boat and run to them, feeling giddy with joy as I have the life squeezed out of me.

"Thank goodness you are all okay," says Mum, "we'll go to Cornwall for our next holiday, and it's safer there!" She gazes at me for the longest time, her face a mixture of pride and worry.

"I wouldn't be so sure about that, Jenna love, our Lottie seems to attract trouble," Dad says as he gives me a massive bear hug.

The fussing and hugging slows down a bit so I wade out to the boat and grab my evidence. Tristan, Katie-Louise and Amy give me a hand.

"Wait till you see what's in the pillowcases Amy," I say to my best friend. "It'll make you laugh out loud for an hour."

A crowd has gathered on the beach. All of the resort guests seem to be here including the scuba diving team and Detective Inspector Bono of the Caribbean Police Force. It's time for Lottie Lovall International Investigator to do her summary, but the Inspector is the first to speak.

"I'm Detective Inspector Bono." He actually holds out his hand for a normal handshake. "I was about to send out the Caribbean Police Search and Rescue Team to look for you," says Detective Inspector Bono. "There's a matter of taking a jet-ski and a dive boat without authorization."

Eeek!

"There was really no need to search for us, Inspector. As you can see we are quite capable of looking after ourselves . . . and solving a serious case. I need to gather everyone together," I reply in my best grown-up voice, ignoring the fact that we are probably in deep trouble for stealing the jet-ski and the boat. A good detective always gathers everyone together. I've seen this on one of my favourite TV programs, *Trouble in Paradise*. "Will you all go to the Sunset Bar and take a seat please." There's a mumble of voices and Inspector Bono looks like he's sucking on a lemon, but everyone does as I ask.

This is a whopping audience. I gaze around the Sunset Bar at their faces. I know at least three people who are in for a shock. I have the turtle shells, the ruby and the pillow cases by my side. With trembling fingers I flick on my phone. My hands wobble and jiggle as I prepare my summing up speech in front of the crowd.

"Hi everyone," my voice comes out quaky-shaky. "I have something very important to tell you about the owner of this hotel, Mr. Hamish MacDougal. He has been stealing turtle eggs and hatchlings to grow precious jewels on their shells." Gasping and mumbling spreads around the Sunset Bar. After a moment I continue.

"I can prove who has been helping him with the trading of rubies and sapphires." It's then I face the guilty one. I turn to meet her gaze. By now her face is the colour of vanilla milkshake and she is picking glittery nail polish from her long finger-nails. "You!" I hold up the picture of the swirly pattern in the sand. "Yes, I'm looking at you Debbie. You left this dainty foot print in the sand when you marked where the turtle's nest was that night." I point at her feet. She stamps them flat on the ground. I'd remembered where I'd first seen that swirly pattern. That day on the scuba dive, Debbie had her feet up on the bench on the boat. I hold the photo of the swirly pattern in the sand towards the police inspector.

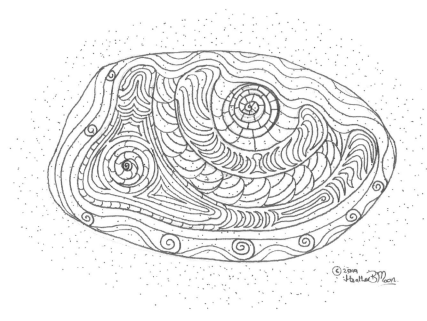

"I think you will find Inspector Bono that this pattern, which I discovered around the turtles nest after it had been tampered with, is the same pattern on the bottom of Debbie's gold sneaker shoe."

Next I hold up the ruby. "And you!" I point at the other guilty one. "I know where you go when the divers are still beneath the sea and the snorkellers are doing their thing. This ruby was found on the beach at Turtle Bay. Rubies and sapphires harvested from the turtle shells are taken by you using the *Highlander* boat which is moored in Turtle Bay. I saw a pile of little bags and fishing nets in the bottom of that boat. The 'important job' you and Debbie do is illegal. You steal the turtle eggs and hatchlings at night time and you collect jewels and bring them to Wadadidili to sell."

Guy jumps up from his seat. "What a load of rubbish!"

"So that's what you do!" Leroy speaks up. "You said you needed to get some phone signal."

"Shut up Leroy! How would you know what we do when you have a nap every time we get around to Turtle Bay?"

My fingers then flick onto the next picture. "This is a picture of the *Highlander*." I hold it up and show it to Hamish MacDougal. "Is this your boat Mr. MacDougal?" He nods his head. I then turn to Detective Inspector Bono. "This is the picture I took that same night, on the shoreline of Wadadidili Beach." I'd also snapped a picture of the two shadowy people going towards the boat. "You will find this boat moored at Turtle Bay Inspector Bono. I'm certain you will find the evidence you need. This boat is used to collect the eggs or any baby turtles that have hatched and scuttled to the sea. You will find nets and traces of containers for eggs in there I'm sure."

Detective Inspector Bono approaches Hamish MacDougal who is still only dressed in his damp tartan underpants and sopping wet furry slippers. "You must accompany me to the station Mr. MacDougal. There are a lot of questions I need answers to. Can someone get this person a beach gown? You two will come too." He points to Guy and Debbie.

"Thank you for listening to my summary," I say feeling proud of myself. Everyone cheers and claps. "Before we go for breakfast I have some presents for the children." I reach into the pillow cases. "Ruby dolls for everyone!" I shout. An excited group of little girls are thrilled with their presents as I share them out. I turn to Amy and whisper in her ear. "No point in telling everyone how a wicked voodoo spell was broken and Ru-B-Loos have returned to their original plastic form."

"No Lottie! Nobody will believe in that mumbo-jumbo. Just don't eat rice with them near you," she jokes.

"Talking about food . . . is the restaurant open for breakfast yet?" I ask, "I'm STARVING!"

"It is indeed," Dad says, "What do you fancy? I know . . . Sausage, pancakes and chips for everyone it is then. It's all inclusive you know!"

* * *

I sneak off after breakfast to see Granny Marley back at her house on stilts. I hand her the Sacred Pendant and with a huge grin she places it safely around her neck. Aztilum, the noble wolf spirit has a canine smile painted across his face.

"Good Voodoolite spirits are all around," says Granny Marley. "They seem to be exploding with delight that the Korecky-Nimo diamond is back in its rightful place and the cosmic powers of the Sacred Pendant are in the very good hands of the Mother of Brightness."

Back in Rainy Manchester

I sit on the sofa watching *Strictly Come Dancing*. Some of the dancers remind me of the Ru-B-Loos. Complete posers with the personalities of lampposts. Pondering this, I wonder what happened to Debbie and Guy.

Dad will be back with the fish and chips soon. Yummy!

Wandering into the kitchen to fetch the drinks from the fridge I glance at the turtle magnet. It will always be a constant reminder of the day I released the jewelled turtles from Wobblite Lake. They are now swimming freely in the wide, wide sea. I smile as I grab the drinks and take them into the sitting room. I remember to snip the plastic six-pack holder before I stick it in the recycle bin. No escaping into the ocean and strangling a poor turtle you horrid-unnecessary-plastic-piece-of-junk.

'Zing Zing!' Yippee! A WhatsApp message from Tristan.

Hope you had a safe trip back.

I have news about Hamish MacDougal.

He's been charged with aiding and abetting in the destruction of the natural environment, cruelty to animals, kidnapping children and handling illegal gems. You provided great evidence with the turtle shells, the ruby and the photos. So, including the evidence on board his boat *Highlander*, I expect he will go to prison for a very long time. He's been ordered to cordon off part of the hotel beach to protect the turtle eggs immediately.

I tap in a reply:

Awesome news! I hope The Creep gets sentenced to at least 10 years in prison.

Tristan replies:

Ha-ha! Probably better than being dragged through that plastic gunge.

I say:

What's happened to Debbie and Guy?

Tristan replies:

They have to do 12 months community service helping with The Oceans' Clean-up Project.

I saw them picking up litter on the beach yesterday.

I say:

LOL! How is Katie-Louise?

Tristan replies:

She's happy because the money made from the jewels will go to Turtle Watch to fund a turtle sanctuary. She says she'll message you now. I'll be visiting the UK next week so we could meet up. Bye for now xx

I say:

Bye Tristan xx

Just as I put my phone down it zings into action again. It's Katie-Louise.

Hi Lottie, Hope Manchester isn't too cold. Wish you'd been here to see Guy and Debbie picking up litter from the beach. It was fun! She may have broken a fingernail already!

I say:

Wish I'd been there. LOL! How long are you staying in the Caribbean?

Katie-Louise says:

Another month then it's back to Plymouth to do my dissertation. It's going to be about the effect of plastic waste on the environment. Also, I need to earn some money so I'll be working with Tropic. I've been talking to Suzie the owner. We have some awesome ideas for the future. The cosmetic company is setting up a 'Return and Refill' scheme. Customers can send their empty bottles to a FREEPOST address and they will receive vouchers off their next purchase or have the bottles refilled for a discounted price. Tropic also have a contract with a major hotel chain to supply little blocks of environmentally friendly soap and shampoo bars which will cut down on all those unnecessary miniature plastic bottles.

I say:

Awesome! Every company should run a scheme like that. Having seen Plastic Island it makes me shudder every time I touch a plastic item now. I counted how many plastic bottles I touch when I get ready in the morning. Shower gel, shampoo, conditioner, toothbrush, toothpaste, face cream . . . it's crazy-mad.

Katie-Louise says:

Yeah! Our kids will live on Plastic Planet if we don't do something about it now.

I say:

Exactly! Enjoy the rest of your time on Wadadidili and I hope you see the turtle eggs hatch.

Katie-Louise says:

Yeah, what an awesome experience it would be to see those tiny hatchlings scramble their way to the sea. Take care, Lottie. Massive thanks to you and Amy for your help. We would never have solved it without you. I still don't believe your story and all that voodoo, mumbo-jumbo stuff though. See you back in the UK! xx

I say:

Hope the duppy bird stays away! See you soon! xx

Dad arrives with the yummy fish and chips. Better help in the kitchen to open them or he will eat half of mine. He still thinks everything is all inclusive!

Facts ...The Boring Stuff! (Maybe not!)

Facts About Turtles

1. Turtles belong to one of the oldest reptile groups in the world – beating snakes, crocodiles and alligators!

2. These creatures date back to the time of the dinosaurs, over 200 million years ago – whoa!

3. Turtles are easily recognised by their bony, cartilaginous **shell**. This super-tough casing acts like a shield to protect them from predators – some turtles can even tuck their head up inside their shell for extra protection!

4. Just like your bones, a turtle's shell is actually part of its skeleton. It's made up of over **50 bones** which include the turtle's **rib cage** and **spine**.

5. Contrary to popular belief, a turtle cannot come out of its shell. The turtle's shell grows with them, so it's impossible for them to grow too big for it!

6. What a turtle eats depends on the environment it lives in. Land-dwelling turtles will munch on **beetles**, **fruit** and **grass**, whereas sea dwellers will gobble everything from **algae** to **squid** and **jelly-fish**.

7. Some turtles are **carnivores** (meat eaters), others are **herbivores** (plant eaters) and some are **omnivores** (a mixture of the two!). Many baby turtles start life as carnivores but grow to eat more plants as they mature.

8. Turtles are '**amniotes**' – they breathe air and lay their eggs on land, although many species live in or around water.

9. These cold-blooded creatures have an incredibly long life span.

The oldest ever recorded, named **Tu"i Malila**, of Tonga Island, passed away at the grand old age of **188**!

10. Sadly, many species of turtle are endangered! **129** of approximately 300 species of turtle and tortoise on Earth today are either vulnerable, endangered, or critically endangered, according to the **IUCN**. Threats include loss of habitat, poaching and the illegal pet trade.

Hawksbill turtles mature very quickly by turtle standards; they reach a length of 24 to 36 inches in **about three years**.

Facts about Corundum

Corundum is a natural transparent material, but can have different colours depending on the presence of impurities in its crystalline structure. Corundum has two primary gem varieties, rubies and sapphires. Rubies are red due to the presence of chromium and sapphires are a range of colours depending on what transition metal is present. and sapphires are formed out of the mineral corundum. Corundum acquires colour when there are other minerals that become present as it is forming. When corundum takes on a hue other than red, the gemstone is typically classed as sapphire. A rare type of sapphire, the padparadscha sapphire is pink-orange.

Rubies and sapphires are rare gemstones that can take millions of years to form. Sapphires are found in recrystallized limestone and rocks that have less silica and a lot of aluminium. When the crystal lattice of the sapphire is forming, if transitional metals seep in, the colour can transform from white and transparent to a different hue. For this reason sapphires are available in various colours. The most popular colour is blue. Since precise conditions need to exist as the sapphire is forming, large gem stones are rare. Over 150 million years ago, rocks inside the earth's surface were subjected to intense pressure and heat to create deposits of sapphire. In most cases sapphires can be found at 6 to 8 miles under the earth's surface. Over time the wearing away of the earth made these deposits more readily accessible to humans. The crystallization of a sapphire is divided into two phases, a nucleus forms and subsequent layers of mineral are added over time.

A Message from Heather

Once again, this story is purely a figment of my imagination. I had the initial idea from the jewelled turtle fridge magnet on my fridge. I wonder why people make fridge magnets of turtles with jewels on their shells. I don't think for one minute the formation of precious stones can be grown on turtle shells. What a horrible and ridiculous thought!

If you have read my others books you will know that I like to weave fact and fantasy together. I would find writing about fact alone would be so dull and b-o-r-i-n-g.

In Lottie Saves the Turtles my main message is about plastic pollution. I think we should all be aware of the huge problem plastic waste is causing our environment. I'm sure you help with the recycling too! Oh . . . and those nasty plastic drinking straws . . . do you really need one? If not, give it back to the waiter or waitress and say,

"No thank you! Have you read *Lottie Saves the Turtles?* Poor Timmy the Turtle has one of these stuck up his nose?"

Happy recycling!

Heather xx

Acknowledgements

I would like to thank all the members of my ARC team and Facebook group 'Super Fans of Lottie Saves the Dolphins.' You rock! Also my 'Awesome Author' friends…you know who you are! If you would like to become a member of my ARC team (Advance Reader Copy) sign up to my newsletter at www.heatherbmoon.com as I send out reminders and information about launching new books and becoming involved.

I must give credit to my editor Rachel Mann, publisher at The Roald Dahl HQ, London. I value your talent and expertise.

As always I am so very grateful to my hubby, Ian for his editing services and constant support.

I love you xxx

About Heather B. Moon

Heather B. Moon was born in Royton, Lancashire and is married with two grown up children and three beautiful grandchildren.

After teaching for some time in the Oldham area, Heather acquired her own school in the north of England. She now spends time at her villa in Lanzarote and walking the South West coast path close to her home in Cornwall.

Heather's passion for animals is greatly expressed in her writing.

'I believe that wild animals should enjoy their freedom and not be held in captivity for entertainment purposes. I also believe in signing every petition there is for banning certain pesticides that harm our insects and birds. We all have a responsibility. Our world is like a tapestry…if one little thread becomes unravelled then the whole planet may fall apart.'

Contact Heather

Sign up for my Newsletter http://www.heatherbmoon.com/contact-me.html

Website http://www.heatherbmoon.com/

My Art http://www.heatherbmoon.com/my-art.html

Facebook https://www.facebook.com/heatherbmoon1

Twitter https://twitter.com/Heather_B_Moon1

LinkedIn https://www.linkedin.com

Praise for Lottie Lovall and Tillie Longbottom

Amazon U.K. : Lottie Saves the Bees

'**My daughter loved this so much she insisted I read it!** As her dad and supposedly 'grown up' I thought it would be to girly and childish. How wrong could I be? The story flows and in between the excitement of the search the book drives home a message we should all take on board. I particularly liked the illustrations and how spooky is the onion man!

Highly recommended.'

'**My children are hooked on this book. A great read!**'

'I loved this book! It's a great story, wonderfully written, fun and very educational. I loved the way the author weaves a very important topic of 'saving the bees' into a great adventure for two friends, a Nan and a professor. You also get to learn a little geography as this book takes you to various countries in Europe as Lottie and her group follow clues hidden in different places. I think every school should have a copy of this book.'

'Great story, great illustration! My daughters couldn't put it down! Was a little too old for my son yet but I'm time I'm sure he will be reading it too.'

'Great wee book, the kids loved it and it helps to make them aware of environmental issues.'

Manchester Special Edition

'Such a fabulous book everyone should buy this young or old. It's great for children and a great way to make them understand how important bees are. The illustrations are superb especially in colour and a great mark of respect made to the Manchester bombings too.'

Amazon U.S.

Loved reading Lottie's adventure in saving the bees. 'What I appreciated about this book was the fact that it

1. Was a great bridge between picture books and chapter books with the illustrations and length of the chapters.

2. Brought an important issue (saving the bees) to life in an entertaining way.

I would like to see a series of these about important issues.'

'Solving a mystery by following clues is certainly a fun part of this book, but what made it most interesting for me was the journey to several different locations in Europe. Also, there are several British figures of speech that are fun to learn about for us Americans.'

Lottie Saves the Bees is available at Amazon

Lottie Saves the Dolphins

Amazon UK

Wow! H.B. Moon has done it again! My kids loved the first Lottie book but they said this one was even better! Lottie is a great character who children will really associate with. The message behind the Lottie books of caring for our wildlife is such an important issue. If you're after a great story line with a strong moral you won't be disappointed. Great read!

This is not the first book by Heather B Moon I have read and certainly won't be the last. I downloaded this onto my kindle the day it was released and decided to read it in anticipation for buying the paperback for my nieces and nephew. By bedtime I'd read the whole book as I was gripped. I love how all the characters and places have a meaning to the author and that it's a topic she's passionate about too. Lottie and her adventures is a fab way for children to learn about how we 'should' be treating animals but with a fictional adventure thrown in the mix. The illustrations really bring this story to life and I personally can't wait for Lottie's next adventure. Amazing read 10/10 from me.

Lottie Saves the Dolphins is available at Amazon

Tillie and the Golden Phantom

It is a real page turner. The main character, Tillie, LOVES horses but her family cannot afford lessons. However she ends up having quite an adventure and achieving her dream in a most magical way. The author skilfully takes the story back and forth through time as Tillie sets out to save a local farm from being destroyed by fire. It's a great read, with a truly entertaining story, interesting characters and a lot of humour.

Tillie and the Golden Phantom is available at Amazon

Printed in Great Britain
by Amazon